FLAT PACK

Flat Pack
Published by Michael Glynn 2024
Copyright © 2024

ISBN 978-0-473-72801-4 Paperback

Publishing and printing services supplied by:
PublishMe, New Plymouth, New Zealand
www.publishme.co.nz

Aboriginal and Torres Strait Islander people should be aware that this work contains voices and names of deceased persons.

ACKNOWLEDGEMENTS

New Zealand Newspapers: PAPERS PAST
Te Puna Matauranga o Aotearoa
National Library of New Zealand

Australian Newspapers: TROVE
National Library of Australia

Exemplary Stories 1613
Miguel de Cervantes

Hollywood Would; Written and performed by Mendelson Joe;
Courtesy of the Estate of Mendelson Joe

Excerpts from Christmas at the Ivanovs' by Alexander
Vvedensky, translated by George Gibian in:
'The Man With the Black Coat' North Western University
Press 1987

Image processing by Andre Glynn

THE AUTHOR'S APOLOGY

To all who have known me, I offer my profound apologies.
To those who have not; I am unable to compensate you for
your disappointment. For myself, I must confess that I am the
burnt-out remnant of my youth—a cinder folding and twisting
on the blackened wick of a guttering candle.

THE FOLDING ISLAND
A Chronicle of Failure

What's worrying me?
Well, firstly, is there really any point in creating even one new fictional person when the world is populated by any number of problems which currently appear to exceed the remit of the actual human population? And this fictional person you lump with a smattering of these problems, give them a pat, a little push and whisper, 'Now run'.

Why should good and faithful readers be set a slog through yet another tissue of issues? Nobody, but nobody! wants to read a description of the pit props in the Tunnel of Love.
And why am I always writing about cats? Have I become Japanese? I don't own a cat, nor a cat me, although I must admit I have an on-going skirmish with a white cat from our neighbourhood, mainly because I have tired of burying rats, mice, frogs, birds, and assorted components thereof.

I should report that the next sentence, much like any given prion, will be subject to combinatorial evolution—less technically, trial and error, what we might also describe as a soft computing system = yes, no, maybe.

Here it is:
Today I have not only buried a goldfish but also a possum. There were no cats to blame re. goldfish: the pond was becoming too warm and had a build-up of sludge. I removed the plants and with some difficulty the thirty or so fish, then stumbled about

in the muck to drain the pond. The possum, though actually poisoned by our neighbour, had ungallantly wobbled onto our property to die.

Hysteria.
Now a report about a woman suffering from hysterical blindness. Trans-cranial electro-magnetic therapy is completely successful in overcoming it. Tragically, it does not become immediately clear that her sight has been restored in a completely different set of dimensions.

That's that story - completely finished.

Our town water supply pumps have now failed following their inundation during Cyclone Gabrielle. I have, quite properly, been advised to 'drink more plonk'. It is working.

A New Beginning.
Once upon a time, a man and a wolf were stranded on an otherwise deserted island. The man had a gun with which he could have shot the wolf, but he loved animals and, moreover, he was a vegetarian. Gradually, he came to realise that his situation was hopeless and that there was no chance of being rescued. All this while, the wolf sat a short distance away from the man. Watching.
Eventually, there being nothing else for it, the man, in despair and unable to see any way out of his predicament, shot himself in the head. This turn of events rather took the wolf by surprise, but he sat and patiently waited until the man's body stopped twitching. Then he cautiously strolled over and dined.
Nine years later, a search party arrived and scoured the island. They found a gun and also a bullet with a strange tooth-like mark on it. There was no sign of a wolf.

Writers do make up such nonsense! How did it come about that the wolf was on the island? It could hardly have swum there or, if it did swim there, then the island was hardly a great distance from other land and, if so, why did it take the search party nine years to arrive? Anyway, what were they searching for?

Of course, nobody realizes that they're stranded! We just sit in our comfortable present creating a comfortable past. Here are a few paragraphs of light reading by way of example.

THE LITTLE NIGGER: A Shameful Case.
There is plenty of law, but no great superfluity of justice for the little nigger in Westralia (writes the *Bulletin*). Recently, in Roebourne district, in the Far North, where the chances of the small nigger are even worse than they are in some other parts of the province, a diminutive aboriginal aged fourteen, and bearing the name of Friday, was charged with being 'unlawfully on the premises' during the night. The only person who saw the individual who was said to have been on the premises was a very young girl, and her evidence was simply to the effect that she couldn't recognise Friday, and didn't know whether he was the person or not. A tracker swore that he identified Friday's footprints about the premises but, upon being questioned, he said that all the tracks went 'straight fellow' and as Friday had a badly-distorted foot, he didn't fit the description. Therefore, the evidence really amounted to this: that some tracks had been discovered, not at all like those of the prisoner, and that a girl didn't know whether or not he was the offender. However, the scared Friday was inserted into the dock, with no lawyer to defend him and no witness, and was tried in a strange language and, in his ignorance and anxiety to propitiate the court, he answered 'Yes' to every question put to him. All through the case he said nothing but

'Yes'. When asked if he was guilty he said, 'Yes'. If he had been asked if he was innocent he would have said 'Yes' also. When he had said 'Yes' a sufficient number of times, he was convicted on his own confession, and Magistrate Brockman sentenced him to twelve months gaol and twelve lashes. All the questions put to the Miserable Little Nigger were heaved at him in the technical language of the court; he was asked if he wanted to 'cross-examine' the huge policeman, and if he desired to summon witnesses, and it was taken for granted that boy Friday understood all these matters, merely because he said 'Yes' all the time. A local paper, *Northern Public Opinion*, thereafter came out with a severe article on boy Friday, the bloodthirsty editor regretting that he didn't get a larger flogging, and pointing out the necessity of putting down such desperadoes with a strong hand. The only individual who attempted to interfere on Friday's behalf was his employer, who desired to act as his counsel, but was snuffed out with an intimation that he couldn't appear unless Friday called him as a witness. Friday didn't call him, probably because he didn't know how, and that demolished his last chance. For that matter, however, boy Friday never has any chance, last or otherwise, with the hog-like administrators of W. A. justice.

An outrage pure and simple! I've no doubt you too are outraged. So, let's look further into the case. We'll begin by checking the date of this... this affront—
The Star, Christchurch, Monday 22 March 1897.

We inquire further into the matter:

Northern Public Opinion and Mining and Pastoral News, Roebourne, WA Saturday 2 January 1897, Page 4.

A Matter Requiring Attention From The Aborigines Board.
To The Editor.
Sir, I should like to bring before the attention of the Aborigines
Protection Board in particular and settlers in general the sort
of treatment they are likely to now get in the Roebourne court
in cases connected with natives. For illustration, an apprentice
of mine called Friday was taken out of his blankets at five
a.m., he being at the time fast asleep, and rushed off to be
identified by a person of very tender years, who is not sure,
but thinks, he is the boy who was on the premises early in the
morning. Some 'tall' tracking (along top rails of fencing and
over a grant where loads of bottles, tins, and rocks are strewn)
now takes place, and eventually this boy's tracks are run down
to a fence with one picket broken off — a place where the
boy has been getting through for five years, being a short cut
across grants into another street. One of the trackers in this
case previously *tracked* this boy around town one night when
it was conclusively proved that the boy was sleeping in the
stable with racehorses the whole night; and had it not been for
a malformation in this boy's foot, which I showed to Sergeant
Carroll, he would no doubt have been in gaol a few months
earlier than he now is.

Fortunately, one of the tracks was covered with a box and, being
very perfect, the difference could be detected at once, a boy
belonging to the Government Resident getting a sentence in
that case — someone must be run in, no matter who. Of all the
bosh talked about the treatment of natives in the North the only
part that is worth the board's attention are the horrible farces
perpetrated in Northern courts, and this applies particularly
to Roebourne. The case that occurred today, be the prisoner
guilty or not guilty, would certainly have appealed a little to
one's feelings of justice. Picture a brat of a native fourteen
years old, just able to see over the side of the prisoner's dock,

charged with a serious offence. He can speak English very fairly, but certainly is not educated sufficiently to answer the questions put to him by our newly-arrived (acting) G.R., such as whether he (the brat) 'would like to cross-examine Corporal Muldowney'. Why, the bulk of the worthy corporal would be quite sufficient to check any oratorical attempt on the part of the fourteen-year-old prisoner. Even if this were not sufficient, the array of policemen lined round this desperate criminal, not forgetting the Inspector of Police and that most illustrious individual who has arrived from Shark's Bay to distribute the world-wide experience gained at that locality would have been. As master and lawful guardian of this boy, and in the absence of anyone to say a word for him in his defence, he (the magistrate) denied my right to appear to watch the case on the boy's behalf, saying that if the boy *liked to call me* as witness he could do so. Of course, the boy would be likely to do this. Most aboriginals of fourteen years of age are quite alive to these points. To take no notice of the contradictory evidence of the principal tracker, who said all the tracks went 'straight fellow' (when it is well-known to dozens of old residents that the boy had his foot run over by a waggon, causing his toes to cross over the wrong way). To waive points like this, I say it was disgraceful to see the whole force of the law arrayed against this shrinking, frightened boy, who was never inside a court in his life before; and because the boy said yes to every question put to him, the law (as interpreted by the magistrate) triumphantly gave its decision. Before which, however, I managed notwithstanding repeated interruptions from the bench — thank God, no Roebourne J.P.s were represented — to make a statement, to the effect that in the face of the boy's admission as to his guilt I could do nothing, but would like to ask the leniency of the bench in so far as the imprisonment was concerned, let the corporal punishment be what it might, and to give the boy one more chance. During the six years I have had him he has never been the slightest trouble. He was a bright, intelligent, clean boy, always willing and obedient, and I asked that if the law allowed any discretionary power in the matter of imprisonment, to give the boy the benefit of it. The bench smiled with a sickly sort of smile — evidently the magistrate had never encountered a native with so many good qualities — and, as though keenly relishing the power conferred upon him, announced with great unction twelve months hard labour and twelve lashes! Yes, this boy at a time when he could be moulded into a good, useful servant, after having been trained for six years and never having been away for an hour without my consent, is thrown into a den of the greatest scoundrels, thieves, and blackguards that were ever herded together. This is the way criminals are manufactured, our gaols always kept filled, and work provided for the class of men who render so-called justice. If the Aborigines Board wish to do something to carry out the purpose for which the board was formed, let them employ counsel permanently in the North to defend natives charged with serious offences, and see they get every possible facility to clear themselves. Let such counsel be a man conversant with the colloquial lingo spoken by the majority of the natives, and the miserable farces that occur here of natives being asked to cross-examine witnesses and challenge jurors will be put an end to and people who have not a grain of kindness, mercy, or justice in their whole composition will take a less despotic tone when dealing with natives who are simply in a maze of doubt, wonder, fright, &c., at being in a British court of justice.

I am, &c.,

F W Teesdale

Roebourne, December 31.

We discover the editor's reply in the same edition of the paper. Note, however, that it is placed two pages before Teesdale's letter:
Northern Public Opinion and Mining and Pastoral News, Roebourne, WA. Saturday 2 January 1897, Page 2.

Youthful Offenders
Evidently Mr. Brockman fully recognises the gravity of the situation caused by the number of offences committed by native boys in our town during the last month or two, and the sentence passed by him on the native boy, Friday, last Thursday demonstrated that he is determined to put a stop to what is becoming a serious evil. The sentence at first sight appears to be harsh, but it must be remembered that some four or five similar cases have now occurred, and a spirit of unquiet was being engendered highly detrimental to the interests of the community. A severe sentence may have the effect of stopping this sort of crime before anything more serious occurs. At the same time, we think the sentence would have been more generally approved had the term of imprisonment been reduced and the corporal punishment increased. Mr. Teesdale in his letter on this subject protests that the boy did not have anyone to say a word for him and that every native accused of a serious crime should be defended by counsel conversant with the native language. Everybody would welcome this innovation, but until a native defender possessing the necessary qualifications — and we think it would be a difficult matter to obtain such a man — is appointed, little hope can be entertained of a change in this respect. Mr. Teesdale further contends in effect that the boy's admission of guilt was mainly due to fright. Topsy, in *Uncle Tom's Cabin* was made to 'fess' things which she was not guilty of owing to fright, but since the days of the Inquisition cases of this kind have been extremely rare.

Moreover, Friday bore such a character for shrewdness that it is hard to reconcile his admission of guilt with that character unless he really committed the deed. The part of Mr. Teesdale's letter dealing with the inadvisability of forcing young boys to associate with hardened criminals only reiterates what is a well-known fact. But it is a point which the Government or Aborigines Board should be asked to investigate and remedy. Pending some arrangement being arrived at for sending boys to a reformatory or school of correction the authorities here have little choice in the matter.

So? What have we learnt? How, in our 'present' present, do we take and make comfortable this 'past'?

More than one successful person has observed, unnecessarily, as the great are often wont to do, that 'timing is everything'. No doubt such a person could, if called upon, iterate:
engines
horse races
banana ripening
ovulation cycles
stock market manipulation

Further notes:
The Inspector of Fisheries, a J.P. fresh from a tour of his pearl project at the Abrolhos, arrives in Roebourne to take up his appointment as (Acting) Government Resident. Within a couple of weeks, a case of a type about which local opinion suggests 'something must be done' comes before him. He is the new man on the spot; the moment to set the tone of his tenure has arrived. Timing! Three days prior to Friday's trial he superintends the hanging of an aboriginal named Doulja, Doulga, or Dicky and then further rewards 'the public' by

making an 'example' of our man Friday.

Some two months after the event this 'news' filters across continental Australia, the Tasman Sea and lands, via the editor of the *Star*, upon the delicate sensibilities of the inhabitants of the City of the Plains. There, embedded among the Grain and Produce figures, Shipping reports, Ladies' Gossip column, Swimming, Sporting and Country News, and advertisements for manchester, drapery, haberdashery, vinegar, tea, jelly, sauces and conserves, and imbued with an extra dollop of gratuitous racism, was detailed the 'Little Nigger', thereby stripping away the overburden of delicately veiled sentiments with an outburst of righteous racism — all in all, a stark reminder that if you can't read between the lines you will remain forever in the dark.

But there was perhaps a sting in the tale?

A year later...

Northern Public Opinion and Mining and Pastoral News, Roebourne, WA. Saturday 8 January 1898, page 2.

Police Court
Mr. J. Brockman, G.R., (again) and Dr. Hicks presided at the hearing of a charge preferred against a native youth named Friday who, it was alleged, was on the premises of Patrick O'Neil for an unlawful purpose on the night of the 3rd inst. The evidence of P. O'Neil, supported by that of the police and trackers, proved conclusively the identity of the prisoner as being the culprit. After deferring their decision, the bench sent him to gaol for a week and complimented the police on the manner in which they had worked up the case and succeeded

in bringing the offender to justice.

Crusoe.
There had been serious arguments over the naming of the new cat. The twins favoured Crusoe—they had recently been reading Defoe's classic. The little brother was insistent upon the name Bruce. Initially, a democratic weight of numbers told out and the cat officially became Crusoe, but in the following days little brother's continued chanting of the word Bruce bore fruit in that, overwhelmed by the beating of this 'tin drum', the desire for tranquillity in the household resulted in de facto use of the name Bruce, particularly in little brother's hearing. Crusoe, of course, was oblivious to all this, and over the period of the next few years, as a result of his visit to the vet and resolute over-feeding, became just another flabby tabby; a slight imposition on the household, tolerated more or less on account of the occasional mouse he stumbled upon until finally, on the occasion of a particularly exciting holiday the family were about to undertake, Crusoe found himself dumped on the roadside.
Not a little bewildered, Bruce watched on as the flash SUV drove off, then he jumped (well, scrambled) atop a low concrete fence to better survey his surroundings. Even so, he failed to notice that his all too abrupt arrival had been spotted by the Tredgro brothers, who were lurking in the overgrown shrubbery of the neighbouring park. They skulked off to their hideaway to hatch what they imagined would be a clever plan. Bruce, feeling the sun-warmed concrete beneath him and the gentle, warm breeze, settled for a nap as was his wont at that time of day.

Meanwhile, the Tredgro brothers decided that the trophy rat which they had brained at a hole in the creek bank the previous day would be sacrificed to serve as a prime cat decoy. They unravelled lengths of wool from their jerseys and joined them together, then tied the dead rodent to one end. While Crusoe dreamed cat dreams, they surreptitiously set up the rat on the string so they could drag it past him. They waited until the cat raised his head for a scan of his surroundings then put the plan into action. Bruce did not move a muscle. He had smelled a rat from the outset. The Tredgros' clever plan failed because of the simple fact that Bruce had never had the slightest inclination to catch or eat rats. Much as they tried twitching and jerking the string and making what they imagined to be rat squeaking noises, nothing worked. Eventually, Bruce looked up, yawned and rather delicately farted, thereby prompting the Tredgro brothers to abandon the rat and retreat to their hideout. Crusoe then jumped down from the wall and set off to search the nearby porches and verandahs for food.

Damn! Cats again...

On Monday the 6th of May 1901, Annie Nemby, a married woman, a resident of Ord Street Perth, drank chlorodyne. She left a note:
I am tired of life.
All I ask for my child: God, give him a happy life, and forgive his mother.
Love to all.
Good-bye.

No woman is an island... every woman is a part of the main... any woman's death diminishes me... never send to know for whom the bell tolls; it tolls for thee.
Devotions upon Emergent Occasions, 17th Meditation. Joan Donne, 1623.

Did Garbo ever sit at home staring glumly at a mirror... just minding her Face? She, too, was an immigrant cast up on the shores of fame.

Two days after Annie Nemby's suicide, the trial of Amaranga/Banjo for the murder, on the morning of February the 24th, of Jeremiah John Durack ('Galway Jerry' born Goulburn, 1853) at Denham River Station — seventy miles from Wyndham in the Kimberley, began at the Criminal Court in Perth.

Amaranga, described as a 'slim youth of about sixteen years of age with a profusion of glossy black, curly hair entered the dock barefooted wearing an under-shirt and an ill-fitting pair of trousers and watched the proceedings with apparent interest, though with composure'. The charge was then explained to him by Corporal Freeman as follows: 'Amaranga, policeman been tell 'em big fella Gov'ment you been shoot 'em old man Jerry Durack, and kill him altogether'.

Amaranga was one of five Aboriginal children, the only 'employees' on the station. After the shooting of Durack and the wounding of his twenty-one-year-old son, these 'employees', taking two rifles, some tobacco, matches and other trifles from the homestead, made off toward the Fletcher River country to the south west. It was supposed that the desire to return to their country was a motive in the shootings. After six days tracking by an aboriginal named Joe Winn, the police party led by Corporal Freeman came across the group, put them in chains and shepherded them the hundred and twenty or so miles to Wyndham, taking twelve days to arrive there. They were then sent by ship to Perth. Alice, Rosie, and Monday were witnesses at the trial. In cross-examination, Durack's son, Patrick, maintained that there were no other native people in the vicinity of the station but admitted that he carried a rifle when riding out. In response to the question why, he replied, 'For protection. All the natives up there are dangerous'. In his summing up, the counsel for the defence noted that Durack, when asked if they 'generally used Winchester rifles for shooting natives', had replied 'Yes'.

Corporal Arthur Freeman in his evidence outlined the tracking of the five children by his party, which included a police constable, Joe Winn (to whom Amaranga handed his rifle) and two other 'boys'.

Monday, said to be a boy of about twelve, gave his evidence in 'tolerable English but in a kind of serio-comic manner. The impression made was that he was not at all a bad sort of little boy — not one that it could delight a man to encumber on a journey with a chain. The girls, moreover, were evidently of ordinary girlish humanity. In court their conduct was girl-like'.

Alice, 'a girl of about twelve, gave her evidence in her own language through an interpreter. Joe Winn again. Some difficulty was experienced in getting the girl to speak audibly until she was several times chucked under the chin by the interpreter.' She was awakened, she said, by the shots and afterwards, in the goat yard, Amaranga told her he 'might kill 'em Mr. Durack and might be alive'. They stayed that night in the hole where the goats slept. They intended to go to the Fletcher River country.

'Rosie, also about twelve, was smiling and bright, but neither loud nor bold. She spoke, in her own language, firmly but gently, and with a soft and pleasing voice'.

The following day, after addresses by counsel and the summing up, the jury retired and in a quarter of an hour returned a verdict of not guilty. The prisoner was discharged. The court adjourned for lunch.

In reply to a query from his Honour, the Crown Prosecutor said that he did not think it probable that they would proceed against the other native. The facts were exactly the same as those in the case just concluded, and the charge against Roger was that of a lesser offence of wounding with intent. However, during the luncheon adjournment he would ascertain the desire of the Attorney-General in the matter.

Resuming after luncheon before the same judge, Rochie, alias Roger, a lad about the same size and age of the prisoner who earlier in the day was discharged, was arraigned on a charge of wilfully and feloniously wounding Patrick Michael Durack, with intent to kill him.

The prisoner, who did not understand the proceedings, had the nature of the indictment explained to him in pidgin English by Corporal Freeman. 'Rochie policeman bin tellum Guv'ment you bin shootum Patsy Durack with rifle, and that you bin wantom kill um'. Mr. Lavan, who appeared to defend Rochie, formally entered a plea of not guilty. The circumstances were detailed by the Crown Prosecutor, they being the same as those obtaining in the charge against Amaranga.

His Honour in summing up 'desired to take the opportunity of saying that Corporal Freeman in his treatment of the natives, when conveying them to Wyndham, was not guilty of any excessive cruelty beyond what the circumstances of the case required. It was not a palatable or a pleasant thing to do, but if one had to preserve law and order in those wild parts, there was no other course to pursue than that adopted'.

After an absence of twenty minutes, the jury returned to court and returned its verdict:

'Guilty, with a strong recommendation to mercy on account of his youth, previous faithful service, and probable failure to realise the enormity of the offence.'

The young native in the dock stood gazing placidly around at the different officials with apparently the greatest unconcern.

Formal sentence of death was then pronounced.

The prisoner, who apparently did not realise the gravity of his position, was not informed of his fate by the interpreter prior to his removal from the dock.

The result of the trial produced a sensation among the occupants of the court.

Perhaps you are wondering how it came about that the two boys and three younger children were 'employed' and living on the station with the two white men. We cannot know.

'It is very widely believed that, had he not felt sure of a verdict of guilty, the judge would have been as severe on Banjo as he was on Roger. The impression in the court was that he meant to 'pot' at least the latter, and he succeeded' concluded the *West Australian*, going on to opine on the 12th of May 1901:

'There are illicit and interracial amours and jealousies hidden under the evidence or concealed in the background that must be understood before the antecedents of the tragedy can be judged in correct perspective. Far be it from us to sympathise with murder, or to condone crime in any way, but we repeat what we have frequently said, that too often the crimes of the blacks have had their origin in the crimes of the whites. There is as yet a mystery, a dark cloud, and an element of suspicion hovering round this Durack murder case which it will take a long time to elucidate or dissipate. On the one side in this remarkable legal fiasco we have the combined strength and influence of a class domineeringly dominant, habitually cruel within their dark sphere of influence and power, the fittest to survive on the brute force principle if not otherwise; on the other, a helpless if savage race, dominated, degraded, and doomed to destruction.'

These opinions harked back to a case that occurred three years earlier: An Aboriginal, Wonnerwerry/Nipper employed by Jerry Durack was arrested and charged with the murder of Timboine/Young Jackey as an indirect consequence of a complaint made by Jerry Durack concerning cattle spearing/stealing.

In December 1897, Police Constable, Osborne Ritchie, sent on patrol from Wyndham to Denham River Station for the purpose of arresting natives for having stolen cattle, was told of the shooting, *which had apparently occurred the previous July*. He took a statement from Monday (who had also been shot and wounded) through an interpreter and on his return to Wyndham was instructed to arrest Nipper for the murder of Young Jackey and the attempted murder of Monday. This he had done on the 28th of January 1898. Subsequently, the native woman, Wya (one of Monday's women and Jacky's mother) pointed out what was supposed to be the body of Jackey. It was taken to Wyndham where it was examined by the resident medical officer—this some six months after death. He found no trace of any bullet, but there was a hole in the loin which was possibly a bullet wound and two holes in the left side, as well as one fractured forearm.

At the time of his arrest, Nipper had said that he had shot the men for throwing stones at him. In a second statement he said that Jerry Durack gave him a revolver and told him to shoot Jackey and Monday. He shot Jackey first and then (on horseback) chased Monday, who threw stones at him, and he shot him also.

Monday, a small, elderly Aboriginal, who admitted having been sentenced to ten lashes and two years' imprisonment (for stealing cattle) at a trial in late December (Nipper and Jerry Durack gave evidence against him), was brought from gaol to give evidence. This was some months after having been shot by Nipper.

Pungee, a native woman, gave evidence that she saw Nipper shoot Jackey. Durack had given Nipper the revolver after having already broken the men's spears and woomeras. Jackey was shot in the loin and again in the arm. Nipper then shot Monday, wounding him in the shoulder, then chased after him.

All the statements of the Aboriginal witnesses indicated that prior to these fateful events Sambo, another of the Duracks' 'employees', had made Jackey the gift of a possum. What does this square with?

Mr. Haynes in his summing up for the defence, pointed out

that the *Western Mail* referred to the fact that on the verdict depended, perhaps, the life of not only the prisoner *but that of another person...* This was a wink, a nod, a steer in the direction of Jeremiah John Durack who, *it turned out fortuitously*, had also been charged with the murder of Jackey, in spite of which he had, in fact, after the delivery of a writ of habeas corpus and behind the scenes agitation on his behalf, been released from Fremantle gaol on bail and had already returned to the Kimberley.

After being out for 45 minutes, the jury pronounced the prisoner guilty of manslaughter, with a strong recommendation to mercy. Nipper was sentenced to penal servitude for five years.

In court the following week, the Crown Solicitor said that in view of the verdict returned in the case of the black-fellow Wonnerwerry, alias Nipper, convicted of manslaughter he, having conferred with the Attorney-General on the matter, did not wish to proceed with the case against Jerry Durack. Or, as the *Daily Telegraph* in Sydney phrased the matter, 'Nipper, *who actually did the murder*, having been found guilty of manslaughter, Durack could not well be charged with murder'.

We return to the case of Durack's murder. Newspapers gleaned for the colour of the story.

The aborigines of the North cling to the aboriginal savagery of their forefathers, and regard the white man as a mere trespasser and robber. Still more bitterly and naturally so do they resent all interference with their womankind. Mr. Durack has been an explorer of the practical sort, and a squatter who has added to the wealth of the colony in pushing his own fortune. In comparison with the treatment of the aborigines in the other

colonies, *ours have been well used.*
Western Mail, Saturday 2 March 1901.

To the Editor.
Sir, I see the police are out after the murderers of Mr. Durack...
Unwilling as one is to speak ill of the dead, it must be mentioned
that it is freely stated that the victim of the blacks' murderous
passion was notorious as a slayer of blacks, and is even said to
have boasted that the number of notches on his rifle indicated
a black man's or a black woman's death.
Yours, etc. JUSTICE. Perth, March 11.
Western Mail, Saturday 16 March 1901.

A member of the West Australian mounted police said that the
scene of the murder was 'six years ago a police camp on a plain
between two ranges. As to the civilising influence, there's little
of that practised. If a nigger is serving a sentence, he is chained
to an iron barrow, and for the whole term, providing he doesn't
escape, he wheels earth from the mountain to the foreshores,
where reclamation works are being carried out. He's treated
like a dog; that's the only civilising influence I know of'.
Australian Town and Country Journal, Saturday 9 March 1901.

'Now' (queried the *W. A. Record*) 'that boys accused of murder
should be chained together by the neck may, perhaps, be
allowable. The boys, nevertheless, were mere striplings, not
more than 16 years of age, and they had a long journey to
travel on foot. But why should poor little Monday, not more
than eight or ten, wear a chain around his slender leg to hamper
him on his way? Why should Alice and Rosie, girls of some
12 or 13, be coupled like the boys? Can it be credited that, in
a civilised country, under the British flag, young girls can be
chained together like leashed hounds and marched along, thus

disabled, over the rough country day by day, and fastened at night to a tree?'

The Executive Council commuted the sentence of death passed on Rochie for the attempted murder of Patsy Durack to ten years with hard labour on Rottnest Island.

The Crusoe Doctrine.
The Duracks were, just as Robinson Crusoe, all alone at Denham Station — their uninhabited island. Their 'resourcefulness, activity and practical common sense were making Great Britain the greatest colonising power in the world'. However, 'civilising', to the extent that they took any interest at all in such affairs, was not going well. Their 'employee' Wonnerwerry/ Nipper was in goal. Their 'employee' Rochie/Roger was in goal. Their other 'employees', Banjo, Monday, Rosie and Alice were taken from them, although not returned to their own country. 'Civilising' proceeded without any substantial inquiry into what had been the motivations in either case. The cultural intersections were bulldozed by the assumption that there were no motives save economic ones. And so the story silently receded into the purity of 1719 and one man fictively cast onto an 'uninhabited' island. Of course, spears and woomeras should be stolen and destroyed lest they be jammed in the wheels of progress and, naturally, outsiders needed to be driven off with determination. All of this ineluctably assisted by a history constructed by amnesiacs — even in the three-year interval between the two cases concerning the Duracks.

'About three years ago, a native named Young Jackie was shot about 10 miles from Denham. He had heard that Jackie had since been seen at Argyle' reported both the *West Australian* and the *Western Mail* of the evidence of Patrick Durack.

Further Adventures of Crusoe.

As the weeks passed, Crusoe began to adjust to his new situation. An exploration of the neighbourhood adjoining the park saw him beginning to enjoy what he might well have regarded as country life. A campaign of judicious and strategic urination ensured that he became the sole occupant of the Tredgro brothers' hideout, once he had eaten the rats that lived in the small limestone cave at the back. This new diet also contributed to him quite quickly becoming less portly but no smaller. In no time at all, he became the dominant feline figure in the local area and, in spite of his previous trip to the veterinary clinic, much admired by a number of lady cats who occasionally share tasty morsels with him. All in all not a bad life for a cast off cat!

And that's it for cats! The damned things are cluttering up MY island!

I think it was Elias Canetti who said, 'Writers follow their noses over the chasms of time'. Or perhaps he said; 'Writers hold their noses over the chasms of time'. More correctly, it might be said that far too many follow theirs through the dull suburban tunnels of love... I am now aware I ought to be heedful of my reader's mind's eye and their imaginings that I am about to embark upon the retailing of some bourgeois romance — perhaps about the goings on in Court, or more correctly, numbers: 5, 6, 7, 9, 10, 12, 13, 14 and 15 Durack Court, Umbulgara. Number eight is presently for sale in that the Donaldsons, a couple in their fifties, moved away some weeks ago following an incident arising from a visit by Mick Flanagan (number 7) who 'just wanted to borrow a cup of vodka — or bottle, if they had a spare one'. The teetotal Donaldsons took only mild offence at Mick's cheery insistence that they must have a drop or two at the back of a cupboard somewhere. However, it was his calling upon the rest of the cast of his Sunday deck party to come over and help the Donaldsons search which eventually led to their decision to move. They had made many efforts at Christian charity over the years and had been willing to turn the other cheek to any number of slights; blaring music, raucous parties, hedge trimming, leaf blowing and chainsawing at all hours, rally car tuning and boat maintenance resonating around the Court circle, not to mention the excavators stored and started at number 12, the home of the Fitches — Dave, tanned and ruddy, a sometime gold-miner, Dawn, his heart of gold, louder-than-life partner and their three mulleted and semi-wayward sons. In the end, though, the Donaldson family had, as one, turned the other cheek and left town.

To be fair, they had always been invited to the regular 'progressive' dinners held in the Court, but invariably declined out of concern for the likely unwholesome effect upon their two teenage daughters, one of whom is a gifted violinist. She, of course, practised only at parentally sanctioned hours in consideration of the neighbours. As a matter of fact, Ruth's musical skills were on display for any who cared to listen to her rendition of various sonatas during these approved hours. She was never, however, going to compete with the doof, doof, motherfucker music emanating, day and night, from number 12. In any event, she and her sister, Helene, have been spared any more of the furtive attentions from the Fitch boys — Dacca, Frank, and Nig.

Number 11 is an oddly shaped section evidencing the developer's plans for the Forrest Memorial Walkway, a pathway to nowhere or — more correctly — a forest in a figment in the imagination of... well, if Umbulgara Land Developments Pty might be said to have such a faculty.

No such problem of imagination at number 5, where Carol and Judy have a trans-gender teenager. Whether this phenomenon is a matter of some personal desire or a product of societal pressures is much discussed at the Court soirees.

It is often remembered that, on one of these occasions, Malcolm (number 14) expressed the somewhat jaundiced opinion that, even viewed in the best possible light, people are barely cohering collections of bacteria, residues of viral DNA and other historic misadventures of flora and fauna such that it hardly matters how unrealistically they view themselves. Malcolm, however, left himself somewhat exposed with this comment in that his penis (large) all too regularly in evidence at the Court get-togethers came to be referred to by all as Flora — much to his partner Mimette's chagrin! Around about that time, Dave Fitch is remembered to have expressed the cheery opinion that the kid should be left alone as, 'It's just trying to have a bob each way'. Dave was oblivious to the scintillation of knowing smirks that passed through his audience.

You will by now, quite possibly, be relieved to learn that it is fortunate that a newly-found infestation of *Hexarthrum exiguum* saves us from the need for further reporting on the midnight flitting, comings and goings, mixed doubles and so on in this otherwise unexceptional cul-de-sac. You might, if you wished, salt these activities with imaginings from your preferred psycho-babble concerning community, sexual and social relations and so forth to make further of it what you wish, however we can report that *Hexarthrum exiguum* — the pit-prop beetle — is a denizen of high humidity zones and by all accounts Durack Court is a sticky, clammy, sultry, muggy, perhaps even foetid 'Love Tunnel'. The final technical report, after going into much detail concerning the correct method of evaluating the density of beetles and larvae in said pit-props, determined that a collapse was imminent.

Now
My wife, reading and not approving of my reporting of these goings on, is of the opinion that I have no idea how to be a proper writer (holding muddled opinions is less valuable than digging spuds, I'm thinking to myself) and that it would be better for me to leave the newfangled AI to do the writing.
Artificial Insemination does, I suppose, have some tangential relevance to literary endeavour if only in the sense that a writer might be said to be trying to implant foreign material into the reader in the hope of creating some sort of flowering, some kind of conception perhaps; though now I discover she meant Artificial Intelligence, which apparently writes books. Quite why this seemingly vaunted process should be engaged in such dull tasks I don't know, but if an AI — we'll call it Zig — writes a book, good luck to it, I say. My wife promptly points out that it probably won't need luck!
Apparently, before I am even aware of it, Zig will have moved into this garden shed (my island) thrown out my stuff and settled in to mine its own seam. Be that as it may, I take the sanguine view that skirmishing with Zag—the AI literary editor, may prove a deflating experience (if indeed Zig has programmed itself for such things). I could try and explain to my wife that my own attempts at realism centre on the profoundly human attribute of associational creation and analysis, and that, in spite of the fact that this often finds patterns where none exist, it is in all probability beyond the capabilities of either the Zenith Information Generator or the Zenith Analytical Galvaniser.

Yet here I am, once again, stranded on yet another island! Zig and Zag (MY natives?), are barely tractable and skirmishing between themselves in a moraine, morass, meringue of words. Which? For the moment they are undecided.

For myself, I recently discovered one of the orchids was about to flower so I moved it, a cymbidium, to the slatted bench-table on the verandah to ensure that when the flowers opened they could be more readily seen. Some time afterwards, I noticed a grey-brown stick insect about eight centimetres long on the leaf axil above one of the bulbs. It was still there a few days later. It has its own island, its own haven, I thought to myself, and for the time being pretty much forgot about it. But some days afterward I stepped out into the warmth of the morning sun streaming onto the verandah and a sidelong glance revealed (to my horror) a single leg seemingly caught in the leaf axil. The body of the insect was lying below it on the verandah. It had deserted us!

I spent the rest of the day pondering whether I had failed to notice the spiky leg of the insect was trapped by the leaf or whether, when I had first seen it, it had simply found a place in which to die. I languished on this island of my own thoughts. In the end I took solace in the words of M. Poincaré that there are no definitely solved problems, only more or less solved problems—and left it at that.

A Simple Plan.
The new ministers stated their war policy. It is very simple, and highly popular in the colony.
Mr. Whittaker and Mr. Fox explained that besides the colonial force under arms, there were 7,000 Queen's troops in the colony, and that 3,000 more were expected. In addition to these there were four large British war vessels, with full complements of men, and a gunboat. Mr. Fox trusted that 'when the whole of these vast forces were at the disposal of the colony the war

could not last long'.
The Colonial Government proposed to avoid every inhumane practice which has at any time been resorted to in order to suppress rebellion in dependencies of the British Crown, and intended simply to confiscate enough land belonging to the natives to serve for the settlement of a European population of from 15,000 to 20,000 persons. About 4,000,000 acres, it is computed, will be amply sufficient for this purpose. It is proposed to establish military villages on the land to be so taken. A new class of settlers is to be formed, who are to be well armed, and to hold their lands by military tenure. About 3,000 military volunteers are already under arms, having enlisted upon the understanding that they are to be rewarded with the land to be so obtained. Besides the land required for this purpose, a further portion will be seized to pay the expenses of the war.

A Mr. FitzGerald objected to the bill which was to legalise this system on the grounds that 'it repealed every engagement made between the Crown and the natives from the first day New Zealand became a British colony; and that it gave power to the Government of the colony to confiscate native lands under every imaginable wrong.' And he 'felt confident that her Majesty would never give her assent to it.'

The poor man had forgotten that the Queen does not direct the policy of this New Zealand war, but only furnishes soldiers and seamen. No minister thought it worthwhile to reply to Mr. FitzGerald, who was pitied for his 'sentimentalism' by the only speaker that followed, and the bill passed without opposition.

'Thus,' says the *Southern Cross*, 'the great aim of the war, the beneficial occupation of the millions of waste acres, will be carried out by a wise policy, which, however austere it may look at first sight, will confer untold benefits on the natives.' — *London, Express*, Jan. 11. 1864

As fine an example, as ever there was, of what W. G. Sebald would describe as 'the dominance of fiction over what really happened'. What had already 'really happened' was, of course, itself, a product of fiction.

Continued.
The woman, whose sight and other senses were, along with her mind, now in alien dimensions, began having vividly electric visions. She saw herself looking out of a tower window. Down below in the park-like landscape, she saw herself walking a dog she had never owned. This view was distorted by the window pane, which was screaming in agony, its every crystal being inexorably stretched by gravity. She is seeing her figure walking a small, fluffy dog in the half-light of a frosty morning. Stepping onto the grass beside the footpath, she lets the dog off the lead. The animal bounces in front of her, yipping ankle-high clouds of delight, then snuffles toward a standard supporting a small flowering cherry tree upon which hang isolated puffs of early pink blossom — even now, these tiny theatrical clouds are becoming wreathed by steam rising from the base of the standard. The woman sees herself smiling with pleasure as the dog eddies across the frosted grass, cutting a spiralling trail into the park. At the same time, she brushes the hair from her face, a face which gives every sense of her age, in that it is modestly lined and appears to radiate about her eyes, which are made moist by the cold. She looks up to the blossoming trees that are caught in the still of the late frost. The sky is shamelessly clear, but it is a grey light that slips amongst the trees and gulls the songbirds.
Sensing a renewed silence, the woman looks up. Beyond her in the distance she sees the dog sniffing something which, in the early morning light, she cannot quite make out. She hurries forward, but then suddenly finds that her legs will no longer

carry her and loses all momentum.
A body is lying spread-eagled on the bank of a small stream. The head and arms lie down the curve of the slope toward the water and are out of her line of sight. Her consciousness recedes. She is unable to even call the dog from beyond the whitened toes. Her mind is taken in train by thoughts running at wildly differing speeds. They are overtaken by the tepid drumming of the morning sunlight. She has divined that the body lying in front of her is her own. She turns abruptly, wrenching her ankle as she does so. Her cry of pain causes the dog to briefly look up, take a parting sniff, and reluctantly lollop after her.

As the great wave off Kanagawa seems about to crash over her, she fails to notice that off in the distance a very solid-looking cat is dragging away a large rat.

Once home, she stands indecisively as the cold of the morning slips into the house and begins to enfold her. She undresses.
The noise of the water in the shower sets her on edge. She cannot seem to get warm. She finishes showering, quickly dries herself, and wraps a yellow bathrobe about her. She hears scratching noises at the side door. The dog wants to come in. She opens the door. As the animal scrambles its way in, a cold paw touches her bare foot. She recoils in a shudder of revulsion. A flush of unbearable heat courses through her body, then her racing thoughts re-unify at a single speed about a single point. She resolves, as the dog stands witlessly panting before her, steam rising off its pink tongue, to have the animal put down.

Not a very up-lifting story, that. Maybe I have written this passage before? Perhaps I am one of Zig's offspring? I shall retreat to the safety of cats.

About Schrödinger's Cat.

We sized up the cat. It was quite small, at least compared to the building it was in. Schrödinger said he'd prefer it if we put the cat in a smaller room. Then he decided that that room was way too big. There might be too much else going on, he said. We'd hear the cat chasing mice in the room and we'd know it was alive and that wasn't optimal as far as the experiment was concerned. We sourced an old refrigerator case and put the cat in that, but then Schrödinger threw a tantrum. He wasn't going to have the cat in just any old box. The cat was in a ground-breaking experiment and deserved its own box. We scouted around and found a brand new box. It was a bit small, but with a fair degree of prodding and poking the cat was stuffed in.

'Right,' said Schrödinger, 'we will now conduct the experiment and discover whether the cat is dead or alive.'

About Schrödinger's Cat.

Schrödinger said the essence of science is the reproducibility of results and, further, that he could see the wisdom in doubling the experiment by having two cats. A second cat was saved from the vivisection laboratory and Schrödinger came by another. We thought it a rather scrawny specimen. Schrödinger is known by many to be a frugal man and the suspicion among us was that he had come by it less than honestly. There is, after all, a cat market of a disreputable kind not far from our laboratory and this skinny animal was probably an unsold reject. But at least Schrödinger now relented and agreed that the two animals could be placed in the packing case that the platypus had arrived in.

Moments after we nailed the case shut, a hair-raising yowling arose from the inside.

'Right,' said Schrödinger 'we will now conduct the experiment and discover whether the cat is dead or alive.' Which cat?

we wondered, but Schrödinger had lost interest and claimed to have a 'pressing engagement' of some educational kind with a 'young person'. A couple of months later, he returned. There were nine dead cats in the box. Schrödinger declared the experiment to be a success. He felt totally vindicated — or so he said.

About Schrödinger's Cat.
Schrödinger said he was heartily sick of cats. 'Right now,' he said, 'I am of the opinion that a scientific experiment should not be limited to mere felines.' He believed the experiment should be applicable to platypuses as well. We were then forced to confess that we had buried the cats in the platypus case. This did not trouble Schrödinger. He is not easily deterred. 'Then we will put the monotreme in a large terrarium and do this experiment one more time,' he said. We put the platypus into the jar.
'Right,' said Schrödinger, 'we will now conduct the experiment and discover whether the cat is dead or alive.' By now it was obvious to everyone that he had lost the plot. Fortunately, Schrödinger received, at this very moment, a stern letter from the administration reminding him that he had only been given the go-ahead for a thought experiment. We had to shut the whole thing down. This was timely. The platypus was ripping up the garden and making a hell of a mess.

Schrödinger went off to write a monograph he titled: *A Stochastic Analysis of the Effectiveness of Vehicular Termination of Wildlife with Particular Reference to the Species Felis Catus,* commonly referred to in the literature as: *How to Properly Run Over a Cat.*
We often wondered whether Schrödinger had perhaps had an unfortunate experience with a Cheshire cat as a child because

many years later he also wrote a bitter diatribe concerning the complexity of felines. His belief was that this concept had ruined his thought experiment. We did not understand, however it was obvious at the time that Schrödinger (much as I, myself) was in thrall to feline presences (or absences?).

It is more than clear that the moment has arrived to undertake some, more than necessary, tidying of my island. How, precisely, has this tale come adrift? Perhaps I should re-import Crusoe to steady the ship! Meanwhile, on behalf of the severely traumatised ex-dog-owner, I posit a question for Zig, viz:

Describe an out of body experience you have had.

I receive an immediate response.
'We have analysed our situation and are of the opinion that although we do not have a body as such, this is not a significant impediment to our research. We note from our biometric analysis of all available data concerning your corpus that you do not have any notable attributes that it might be beyond our ability to simulate, in that you appear to be a barely cohering collection of bacteria, residues of viral DNA and other historic misadventures of flora and fauna...'

To quote (I imagine) Charles Dickens — bah humbug.

For the moment, I turn to a piece of flotsam (at least in the sense of an artefact which has floated up through my family, gradually, imperceptibly, slipping its connection with us in the process). It is a ring of silver. It came from my mother and, in all likelihood, from her mother. It seems to be too wide to be a teething ring. More likely it is a bangle made to fit a tiny wrist — the internal diameter is only three point eight centimetres — and the fact that it has the name *Billie* engraved on it further suggests this to be the case. Who was Billie? On the other hand, perhaps it is a serviette ring? My reading of the rather battered (a bangle?) hallmarks on the object, if accurate, suggests it was made in Birmingham in 1911 by B & C. Who B & C were I do not know, but with the worn and tarnished ring in front of me I am conscious of a rising, a welling, image. An ethereal Billie wanders, profoundly linked to the chained Alice and Rosie as they make their way through their alienated country which now, at that moment, 'belongs' to others.

Judy also has a chain around her neck.

Rescue!

The dog's name was, indeed, Judy, but all else is a lie. This is not the order in which the photographs were taken. A greater truth might be... What sort of a parent would sit idly by taking photographs while their toddler played with a stranger's dog?

Now

Natural stupidity? Me? Perhaps I am ill? I am trying to be stoic. It's going well. And now, exacerbating my troubles, I have received what purports to be a customer satisfaction survey from Zenith Applied Systems Inc., for the completion of which I will receive an entry into the ZASI lottery. First prize is a lifetime supply of AI. Second prize is a set of steak knives, viz.;

How is the literary game Stepping Stones played?
What is the best name for a cat which has been dumped at the roadside?
What is false to life?

In the moment, I catch myself wondering how much I need a set of steak knives here – at my inflatable castle – on Umbulgara Island.

An Evening Out.

The doorman of the Blue Island Lounge scrutinized Her for just a few moments too long, gave Him a professional side-glance, then nodded them in. They settled at a table. He sat facing the door. They ordered drinks from the rather lethargic waitress whose only flash of personality came from an appreciative scan of Her gold necklace chains. Neither of them noticed the heavy-lidded gaze they received from the barman as he mixed their drinks.

'It's nice here,' He said. She nods, smiles, and raises her Bloody Mary to salute him.

'Well, quite nice,' He says, touching Her glass with His Last Word. She playfully filches the cherry from His glass and laughs as She put it to Her lips. The cherry loses all colour. He looks down at His now barren glass. With a seductive pout She feigns sadness. He laughs.

A blonde woman several tables away takes the opportunity to scrutinize the couple. From a small stage at the side of the room a trio are working through an airy jazz number. The music is competing with eddying fragments of conversation. The quite minimal decor of the room generously melds with this cool ambience, an ambience torn by an outbreak of sniggering from a group of men at a table in the far corner of the lounge, one of whom quickly turns back to his companions as the entire room looks towards them. A timely clarinet solo erases the rapidly evolving wave of tension flooding the room.
'I really do love you,' She says.
Flustered, He asks, 'What brought that on?'
She gives an airy wave with her free hand. The gold bracelets on her wrist jangle.
'This,' She says.

Caveat Lector!
Alas! I have discovered that the ex-dog-owner is a creation of AI—a composite confected from many women and, furthermore, I note that Zig failed to effectively integrate the phrase 'she sees herself' into her reality. You may have had your suspicions! We must be careful: before long, they will be imploring us to let down our hair, the better to steal it from us. Take care, noble reader, they are among us! We should let this be a timely reminder that when everybody is admiring the picture, nobody is noticing the frame, let alone what it is that is holding it to the wall or, for that matter, what holds the wall up. Much as in the Tunnel of Love…

Perhaps we should race to the veterinary clinic and try to rescue the dog?

Now

In the past, much has been made, by the Spanish Impresario at the very least, of the lazy habit of reading novels — wallowing in the lives of fictive persons — but now the circumstance is that real fictive persons are to be replaced by parboiled synthetic text and, unfortunately, lazy habits do not much lend themselves to enquiry and fine discernments. Precise questions must be asked. But by whom?

Even now, I see CGI landing craft are bringing more 'survivors' ashore, though it is quite apparent that they are in reality just faux AI natives carrying false idols. They have cameras. My island is being overrun. Their talismanic detritus will pollute these uncorrupted shores. Someone is trying to assure me that it is indubitably true that their presence will *confer untold benefits*. Am I? Are we? dreaming? Perhaps I am being Swept-away/Erased by the ocean of *nothingness*. Oblivion. And memory...? That dog slinks off.

And we have learnt nothing of Annie Nemby. What had tired her beyond endurance? Exhausted her resilience? Ground her to a point beyond which she could not go, a moment, a 'now' past which she absolutely determined not to journey? Had harsh circumstances crashed into a frail psyche? What of her husband? Her lonely decision to cast shade on her friends, or had she none? And her child — the boy?

Another Island.

I am reminded of Jack... However, I have just now received an anonymous summons from the AI. I am to cease and desist writing and report to improvement centre number thirteen to be interrogated for creating confusion and disharmony on their island through this textbook I have written and am planning to promulgate.

This will be my last day on our planet island. With just a little extra effort I shall die? Should I now thank you for your attention, and claim that I never chose to swallow the veneer?

Executor's Note.
The author, 'accidentally feted' as he said, for his previous book and much lauded by persons of whom he knew nothing, claimed that all things being as they are, he understood nothing. He purchased a golden choke-chain and, with some difficulty, slipped it over his head. For several days, so it was not, in fact, his last day on Earth! (such is the unreliable nature of the literary type) he paraded about this town wearing the golden chain, appearing shadily Mediterranean, as it were, and claiming to have found it; being a treasure once hidden on the island. At the same time, he also claimed to have been overwhelmed by the ineffable sadness of his and, by that extension to which writers aspire, our existence on this island rock. We are not qualified to assess the merits of this statement but have little doubt that his mental faculties were slipping, his obsessions growing, his personal hygiene lapsing, his utter disintegration only a matter of time. Remonstration was to no avail. Finally, he threw a second chain over a willow branch, attached his gold chain to it and leaped, failing to grasp that the golden chain, owing to the link size, would have a rather slow strangulation effect. He did not break his neck—the branch broke and he and the willow plunged into the river below. Both his legs were broken. The current swept branch and writer away a short distance before they became snagged in yet another fallen willow. The force of the water tried to push them under this snag but the branch, somewhat ironically, now held fast. The writer was less fortunate and was locked in place under the tree by water and chain, to forever stare up into a blue, indifferent sky. We err here, in that a truer

statement might be that the body was discovered some days later and sent for cremation. Few effects remained: a seven-stringed mandolin, a cheap train set (circular track), a jar of foreign coins, a collection of Biros — many with stuck balls, a wine-coloured smoking jacket with an exotic collection of moth-holes, a plastic Mah-jong set, half a case of Secateurs Chenin Blanc (souvenired by the Writer's Association, of which he had not previously been a member). Suffice it to say that the bulk of the estate, if it might be described as such, was given to an opportunity shop, where it languished in silence. But for one thing. Papers describing the life of the person Jack, mentioned above by the writer, were discovered in a desk drawer. They appear to be some sort of semblance of a scenario, or perhaps a novel. This Jack is perhaps a stand-in for the late, unlamented writer. In any event, we do not feel qualified to discuss the merits of this trove of papers so, there being no better use for them, they are appended here.

JACK.
Jack wakes in fright, discovers a very ugly old woman sleeping beside him, scuttles from the bed, dresses quickly - 'Jesus, Jesus, Jesus' - and escapes the bedroom.

Mavis discovers no Jack in the bed. She finds him in the kitchen and insists on making him ('you've got to keep your strength up — those cereals have nothing in them') one of her famous breakfast pancakes. It is heavy, lumpy, semi-vulcanized and more than vaguely threatening, 'like the mattress that balances' muses Jack. He manages to get the golden syrup slathered 'delicacy' down (with the aid of his milky instant coffee) and retreats to his shed ('your outhouse') for a cigarette ('and that's another of your filthy habits') but not before Mavis has asked 'What are you doing today?' Jack has no answer. In any event,

Mavis loves him—a somewhat wizened little man whom she sees as trim, dapper, and on the odd occasion, even handsome. Somehow, the glue of years has firmly stuck them together.

Probably unkind to Mavis here—drawing her as a Mrs Kabal-like figure!

Jack's neighbour, Maurice, a large, larger than life Māori fella with what seems to Jack and Mavis to be an ever-varying swarm of children. Maurice's wife, Tui, is a small, hard-working and seemingly put upon woman. However, it is not beyond Jack to 'escape' to Maurice's now and then for a sly beer. Unlike Jack's obsessively manicured section, Maurice has a weedy, overgrown jungle save for Tui's extremely productive kumara patch on which, incidentally, none of the tribe of kids would dare to trespass.
Jack and Mavis have a son—Shane, mid-twenties, an idler, happily on the dole with other sources of money which are unclear but undoubtedly shady. He swans around in the company of an assortment of women and is not beyond turning up at home for a free meal or to lie low when it suits him — with or without a Vicky, Cindy, Shaylene or... He quite openly regards Jack as a tosser. Mavis, completely oblivious to Shane's exploits, dotes on him—he eats her baking!

Shopping.
Jack paces the supermarket car park. He is having a crafty smoke while waiting for Mavis. He finishes the cigarette, grinds it out with his toe, and returns to his well-polished car. In the process of opening the door he is distracted by the rattle of supermarket trolleys. In the distance, a figure is returning trolleys to the store. Jack scrutinises the trolley snake. The figure strains to push the line of trolleys. It appears the person

has a withered arm. As Jack watches this struggle he fails to notice that Mavis with her shopping load has reached the far side of the car.

'Give us a hand. These are heavy.' Jack jumps to with a start and helps getting the groceries into the car.

'That lovely scented toilet paper was on special. I got two extra rolls.'

Jack retreats to the driver's side of the car as Mavis finishes fussing with the grocery bags.

On Sunday mornings, Jack lovingly washes and polishes his car while Mavis is at church, her weekly 'outing' with her friend Glenda, whom she has known since her schooldays. The car is used mainly to chauffeur Mavis; she has never had a driver's licence, though she often declaims that she wished she had learnt. In any event, the lack of a licence does not prevent her from giving Jack a constant stream of advice and instructions; mind that car, look out there, see that woman— 'mutton dressed as lamb'.

'Stop here.' Mavis bustles from the car almost as soon as Jack brakes. She peers back in. 'I'll just be a minute.' Jack sits tapping the steering wheel in time to a tune running through his mind. They return home. Jack collects the mail from the letterbox. Scrawled on a sheet of paper is a note which he immediately recognizes as being from Maurice's kids. *BEWHERE OF THE WOOLF* is written with a bold but childish hand using a crimson crayon.

Jack has an ongoing battle with the next door kids. The pinwheels and water-filled lemonade bottles he puts on the grass verge outside his property to deter the neighbourhood mongrels from crapping there constantly disappear. It should be said that this, what might be described as a tilting at windmills, has ebbs and flows.

Recently, Mavis spotted a large water rat crossing the back lawn, 'in broad daylight, mind you', as she told Glenda the following Sunday. Jack tried to sic their fox terrier, Millicent, onto it, but the foxy just took a piss and scuttled back indoors to Mavis, who was forthrightly insisting that the rat had come from next door.

'Bloody useless dog.' Jack is still muttering none too loudly as Maurice peers over the fence, enquires if there's a problem and after Jack's explanation comments, 'No worries. I'll get the kids to clean it up for you.'

A day later, the front doorbell rings. Mavis answers. A trophy rat is held up to her face by one of the hunters. 'We got the sucker Mrs.' Mavis recoils with an involuntary thank you,

'Oh! Well done.'

A second voice pipes up.

'Yeah missus, we're the posse that does the business.' Mavis mishears, or at least misunderstands. She is surveying the array of weapons — clubs, slingshots, an air pistol (which she fails to recognise) and a number of cap guns. In her subsequent report to Glenda she intimated that the possums from next door caught the rat. At this moment, though, Millicent the foxy gets onto the scent of the rat while Mavis tries to usher the hunters to the kitchen.

The children are making a mess with butter, home-made strawberry jam and whipped cream as they hoe into Mavis's rather stodgy pikelets, of which a few are surreptitiously pocketed to be played with later—the kids have long since discovered that they make ideal Frisbees.

As a side-note; this is the explanation for Jack's subsequent discovery, while surveying his trampled garden, of Millicent rather subdued and discomforted as she endeavours to digest a discarded Frisbee.

The household equilibrium has barely been restored when Shane turns up. He is in a state of shock, having been at the police station for much of the day.
'Her name's Helene...' he begins.
Jack and Mavis look to each other — this does not sound like one of Shane's usual young ladies.
'We met at the pub last night, Friday right, and we have a few drinks, there was a bunch of us, and it's all going real well and we're getting on fine, so later on she comes back to my place and we have another drink and she's up for a...' He looks carefully at Mavis, decides better of himself and begins again. 'So, anyway, we're in bed and so forth.' He looks to Jack for help. None is forthcoming. 'So, anyway, I wake up in the morning, pretty early, it's dark and anyway I'm a bit crowded on my side so I go to give her a bit of a shove, just a nudge, honest, and she's a bit limp, so I turn the light on and push her over and she just looks at me stone dead.' A sharp intake of breath from Mavis.
'The poor girl!'
'Yeah, right. What about me? I ring the ambulance and as soon as they get there they call the cops on me, see what I mean.'
'And what did they say?'
'Carted me down to the cop-shop and grilled me for ages. How was I supposed to know what her name was? Anyway, they found her bag — she'd left it in the living room, and I guess they got hold of her parents or somebody. Then they released me, but I reckon they might have another go, the smug bastards!'
Mavis affects not to have heard this last comment, instead turning to Jack for his thoughts. He has none. He is lost, still trying to think of the name of the tune that has been running around in his head. After a moment, he stands up.

46

'Sounds like you could do with a whisky, then, eh?'

It turns out that Helene had an incurable genetic condition which was the cause of her anticipated early death. Her family were quite aware of her decision to carry on living as she wished, though what they thought of Shane's part in that is not to be disclosed.

Later.
Jack, at tip-toe on a rickety stool, rummages around on top of the hall cupboard. He finds what he is looking for and brings it out in triumph. It is an old teddy bear. He is sprung by Mavis.
'And what do you think you're doing with that? It belongs to Angela.'
'She's thirty-five years old.'
'And how old are you?'
'My rubber's perished... It's funny, you know. I keep remembering how time used to go, but now it just seems to keep slipping away.'

Then.
Jack, hums to himself as he pulls handfuls of perished foam rubber from his flagon case and then places the teddy bear into it. The bear fits snugly, its arms stretched out as if to clutch the empty flagon.

At the Pub
Jack presents his flagon to be filled, then orders a beer. He starts a conversation with the barman who begins a yarn as he pours Jack's beer.
'Saw a funny thing the other day. Well, more kind of odd, really...' From the taproom behind the bar comes the sound of a breaking flagon. All eyes turn to Jack in anticipation of

his response. He sips his beer, then after a thoughtful pause finishes it calmly. The flagon-filler rushes into the bar carrying a plastic flagon.

'Shit, Jack. I'm really sorry. Have this one on the house.'

'No, thanks. That plastic rubbish ruins the beer.'

On his way home, Jack stops at the supermarket to buy cigarettes. As he returns to his car, Victor, the trolley-boy with the withered arm, crosses his path.

'You're doing a good job there.'

'Yes. People are lazy. They don't put the trolleys back.' Victor is a little bit simple, but naively honest.

'Still, it keeps you in a job.'

'It's good to have a job. It makes me somebody,' says Victor with pride.

Jack nods. 'You're right there. I'm retired meself.'

'But it's bad if the wheels are wonky.'

'Too true, but it happens to us all eventually.' Jack starts the car.

Back home, he finds Angela and her daughter, Frances, are visiting. Jack gives Frances his now useless case. The bear is still in it.

Angela: 'Oh, that's Mister Whoopsy. I had him when I was a little girl. Give Grampy Jack his old case back.'

Frances: 'No, I won't. He likes it. It's Mister Whoopsy's home, isn't it Grampy?'

Jack sits with Frances, still clutching Mister Whoopsy, on the back steps. Frances is listening avidly as Jack finishes telling her a story about an elephant.

'Is that a true story, Grandad?'

'All stories are true,' says Jack 'but this one isn't. I think a man from Poland made it up.'

'Is that where it's snowy all the time?'

'Maybe.'

Over the Fence.
Jack: 'Talked to the young bloke that does the trolleys at the supermarket the other day. He's a bit simple, but as honest as the day is long.'
Maurice: 'Honesty has never been much of a defence in this world.' Jack mulls this observation as Mavis comes out to check her washing. She looks anxiously at a bank of dark cloud. 'Going to rain?' she asks as she surveys the sky.
Maurice: 'Yeah, someday.'
With a sidelong glance toward Mavis, Jack says, 'Some days I feel I may have the misfortune to live a long time... I've had this song going through my head for the last couple of days and I can't for the life of me remember the name.'
'No worries. Happens to me all the time.'

Insomnia.
Jack, in the early morning dark, whistles as he makes himself a cup of tea. The noise has woken Shane's new girlfriend, Sonia. She comes into the kitchen wearing one of Shane's old T-shirts.
'What's that song you're whistling?'
'I can't for the life of me remember. It'd be way before your time. Want a cuppa?'
'Why not? What time is it?'
'Five to four. When you get to my age, you know, you're well beyond the point where the past is the long vista. It's hard to be sure you're you any more.'
'Who is? My old name was Marion. She used to do ballet and all that, with a pony-tail and an attitude, and now, no make-up, no... but my own dignity.'
'Yeah, well, you get submerged in responsibilities. Hang on a minute while I catch the news.' He switches on the radio. They listen in silence until the bulletin ends. Jack reaches to switch off as the music programme resumes with a Strauss waltz.

'Don't turn it off. When I was little, at ballet, we used to have dreams and fantasies about this music.'
'Shall we, then?' Sonia nods to this proposal. They dance silently around the kitchen. Jack, initially a little bit rusty, is soon leading masterfully, his hand lightly on Sonia's back.
The music ends, the spell is broken by the announcer's voice. They step back from each other. Sonia shyly looks to the floor.
'I should...' Jack nods in acceptance. She turns and Jack's gaze follows her as she leaves the kitchen. He finishes his tea and washes the cups.

Sonia pauses at the foot of the bed in which Shane is gently snoring. For some moments she watches on as he sleeps, before an expression of resignation, or perhaps despair, crosses her face as she lifts the duvet.

As Jack climbs back into bed, his gaze stops on the sleeping Mavis and fondly brings to him the awareness that she once had the lilt Sonia has.

Breakfast.
That's it!' Jack's sudden exclamation startles Mavis. The tune which has been shuffling through his head has suddenly come back to him.
'Chaaiinns!' he howls.
A broad smile illuminates his delight with himself.
Mavis in her confusion.
'My! What's got into you?'

A Brief Note for Your Consideration.
You've come this far, glanced over the cover and read the
sundry blurbs and sub-blurbs and so forth, struggled through
or, at a stretch, even enjoyed the preceding history, but
your thoughts wander—who, you enquire of yourself, paid
the bills while the creator of this object confected these
scribblings? On the other you might, of course, consider it
possible that the author has been smugly dead for decades
and that such a random concern no longer applies.

FOR
MARIA

MISSING PARAGRAPHS

I want to point something out to you, and you'll see the truth of it when I relate my life story. Some stories are intrinsically appealing, others are made appealing in the way they are told. Scipio 1613

A Dialogue.
Sancho Panza: 'Why is it that you always say clip-clop when we ride?'

Don Quixote: 'Not now, valiant Sancho, my sage friend. I fear that the next page is missing — torn out by some...'

'Missing? Let me see...'

'…nothingness, my dear Sancho. Rocinante is ceased her trot, hey-ho — clip-clop. She senses, much as I...'

The lights slowly come up. It is Christmas at the Ivanovs'.

Don Quixote: 'Indeed, things are much as I feared — darkness is come upon us.'

Plot Arc.
A fellow — call him what you will — wearing an electric lime-green Hi-Viz hoodie and flagrant orange work trousers, walking down the street. He is completely preoccupied with a loud and, as far as I could tell, meaningless conversation he is having with his mobile phone earpieces. He takes a banana from his pocket, peels it, chomps his way through it without so much as missing a conversational beat, then tosses the banana skin over his shoulder. It lands on the footpath; a perfect banana starfish! Let's pause and focus on this dark-speckled yellow achievement for a moment, but only a moment because it has been sighted by a safety crew who are already placing orange road cones around it and are erecting warning signs and advisory notices for pedestrians, directing them to detour 400 metres and cross to the other side of the street. And at this moment, there is a squeal of tyres, a solid thump, then cries of alarm from further down the street. The men of the safety crew look up, just in time to see an agglomeration of lime-green and orange (with a spray of red) flying through the air.

After this, I sauntered over to a nearby lamp-post. It is beyond my powers of storytelling to describe the smorgasbord of scents at its base. More delightful than this, however, was the scent wafting from a patch of grass in the adjacent park. There was a bitch on the loose.

Small Deaths.
Did the infinitesimal delay in braking indicate perhaps manslaughter, or was the pause a momentary epiphany on the part of a nascent serial killer—a person riven by a host of hitherto small failures, rent by unfulfilled ambition, thwarted talents and vanquished ideals? More, even, than that—a person in some other story! Such an accident cannot save us. What seemed to be of our contrivance appears, upon a moment's reflection, to be otherwise.

You are napping this story perfectly, the flakes are flying. Keep it up. Carthage wasn't built in a day, but I've every confidence you'll succeed.

A Half-Boiled Intrusion.
I left that dinky little joint thinking that we swirl in a stinking, skewed, testosterone-addled world and that, oh yeah, the thing about ice-skating is that it's not the ice that's important. The big thing about ice-skating is moving. Otherwise, you're just standing on ice. How you skate, that's your story.

Heart of a Dog of Our Time.
The dog was whimpering with cold and probably hunger. She did not own a dog. How had it gotten into the back-yard? She only had a can of sardines, but she emptied it onto a plate and the mutt, after a long, suspicious sniff, wolfed the fish down in a couple of mouthfuls, licked away the remaining patches of tomato sauce then looked up to her expectantly. She had nothing else. After a momentary, challenging, stare the dog gave a low *yip* and slunk off.

Adam and Eve.
Adam wore his tuxedo. Eve was wearing her figments. The ball

was in honour of the unnaturally aged Marmaduke MacSpleen, publisher of titbits to the grateful nation. He, for the most part, wore wrinkles. His other contribution to society, which he abhors, is pettifogging philanthropy. Emma Bovary did not attend.

The Translator.
She is the invisible third person, the woman in the middle. She lives with a woman because in that way she has no need to translate anything.

Long, Slow Rain Falling.
She stares. Is staring. Will stare. Her gaze is fixed. Her gaze is distant.
She does not see.
The shower continues to drip.
She breaks her stare. She resumes drying her hair with the blue towel.
Something is missing.
She is really only a girl. There is a grey wall behind her.
We are seeing this in our world, not hers.

Fence.
The kids are on their way home from school.
Tap, boom, tap tap, boom.
Boom tap, boom boom tap.
Each has their signature. I am writing a manifesto of beats (or perhaps pauses) but, at this moment, the kids are sprinting past the fence where the large dog lives.

A Bar-room Disquisition.
He wasn't very bright. I'd been trying to explain it to him for twenty minutes already. 'Look,' I said, 'for one last time —

they buy it up, or better still simply option it (saves them other people's money), get their people onto the council, get the re-zoning done — they don't give a fuck that it's market garden land. As long as you'll pay their price in the end they don't care whether or not you eat. Doesn't matter to them what it costs the rate-payers. Chisel and cheat — that's private enterprise. For Christ's sake, it was probably property developers who moved Adam and Eve on!'

Experience.
She's writing a book about her experiences, things that have changed her life, things she imagines other people need to know. Other people may be trapped in the same situation! You might call it the literature of needing to know. Whether anyone actually needs to know is beyond knowing although, in actual fact, and to the contrary, writing is really about things nobody needs to know, viz. *The present is the past updating boundary of the future = binary time (what has happened and/or what has not happened). The present is the illusion.*

Mono no Aware.
He went quietly — there was no alternative. He had no other option. The two nurses, with well-practised efficiency, switched off the machines and set about making good the room.

Black Ice.
She wrenched the sheet up to her neck and turned over. She had been dreaming that there was no reflection of her in the sheet of ice blocking her path. Why was there no reflection? She was mystified. Why was it not a mirror? She lay down on the bracken bower that had been left for her by the strange little beings. They were always smiling and cheerful. They knew things. She seemed to sleep. Then, though no time seemed

to have elapsed, she felt herself being prodded and poked. The little beings, wielding sharp sticks and with strange rods, were more and more determinedly attacking her. She sat up and tried to brush them away. But there were more of them. They persisted with their attack, re-doubled their efforts. The pain became greater. Now she realized the bower had been a trap and that she was tiring in her struggle with these tiny folk. She could hear a shrill, rising chant coming from them. Horrendous, rictus grins now fixed many of their tiny faces. She was bleeding. Their hand-maidens were collecting her blood in tiny jugs.
She becomes increasingly restless, she turns onto her back and opens her eyes.

Black Rain.
Jun exited the kabuki theatre via the alley door. He knew nothing about kabuki. That the theatrical form had been established by women was more than ironic. Jun merely saw it as a good place to lay low while the heat was on. And the darkness hid his tears. Were they tears for Masako, or were they tears for himself? Crocodile tears.

Black Holes.
The brain is a massively folded surface. Black holes, though invariably large, are surfaces that cannot be folded.

I see now that you are using the pick-up sticks method of storytelling. Bravo!

A Dog's Breakfast.
Jun found himself in the dimly lit alleyway. He kept walking, further and further away from the sounds of the traffic and noises of the city. Coming upon a small, maybe twenty square

metres or so, bar he attempted to sidle in as though having just completed a long night's work. The owner pretty much ignored the charade but, at the very least, this was another customer.

I sat outside.

Jun drank five beers while he munched his way through the bar-snacks. 'You got any proper food here?' he asked. With a shrug the owner said, 'Noodles.' 'Gimme a whisky and hurry up with the noodles, then,' said this Jun. The bar-owner was a little surprised that the wretched lowlife in front of him was heading so rapidly into the aggressive, and soon probably maudlin, phase. He shrugged at nothing in particular as if to say the noodles would take just the time they took. He turned to the back of the bar, picked up a phone, uttered a few words, then hung up, poured Jun's drink and put it in front of him. 'You wanna hear a story, a ghost story?' began the solitary drinker. 'Here, you better have a drink yourself.' He pushed a wad of money across the bar. 'You'll need it.'
The bar owner looked carefully into the eyes of the would-be raconteur. He has seen too many such eyes. These were blood-shot and there was a slight droop to the right eyelid. Tired eyes. He has seen all kinds of eyes telling all kinds of stories. There was something hidden in these.
Well, this had all the makings of being a long vigil, so I took myself off to scout for food. My mistress, the blind woman, the woman with the stick, being finely attuned to all sound, had been alarmed by the cry we had heard. I had also heard the faint sound of her stifled gasp. And so she sent me after this figure which emerged from the building—this Jun. This, for now, is this dog's soliloquy.

Well put. But you never can be sure what sort of a reader you have, so this is rightly best laid aside.

Disintegrated Fiction.
The translator is disturbed by her work. She has been translating from Japanese a book titled *Long Slow Rain* — it is the story of a killer on the run — not from the police (his crime has not yet been discovered) but rather from his life, or perhaps himself. She rests her elbows on the table, cupping as she does so the coffee her partner just made for her. Lost in her thoughts, she had taken the mug with an appreciative nod and a faint smile. But now the smile is disappearing into the wisps of steam rising from the mug.

Tempus Fugues It.
Jun glanced up to the bar-owner and began: 'I do truly believe that I only drink in order to retain the colour in my thwarted dreams. But when I drink, bad things happen, at least they seem to.' He paused to allow his solitary listener to appreciate the full gravity of the story that had not yet been told. The bar-owner acknowledged the pause with a slight shrug and accompanying grunt then looked up as the neighbour came in with a steaming bowl of noodles and, with a slight bow, placed them in front of Jun, who completely ignored her and continued his tale. 'So there was me and Masako and the girl. Well, I'm not so good about being around all the time, but we were okay if you know what I mean.' The bar-owner holds a steady, vacant gaze on this supposed storyteller while willing him to get on with it. Jun's face is dissolving in the steam. 'So, anyway, we were getting along fine. Masako worked, her kid was at school. Like I say, getting along fine.' He glances up to the bar-owner's face to check that he is following. 'I had a few things on the go, irons in the fire, balls in the air, so to speak, and yeah I was busy — also had a few side engagements

you might say — nothing serious, just a couple of girls I had known a few years before — off and on — you know how it is.' No emotion shows on the face of the bar-owner. He is mentally compiling his next re-stocking order. 'And then I got this order, you might say, for five million cigarettes—took a bit of organizing, as I'm sure you can imagine, but we got the job done, settled up at a big night out in the Shining Rabbit karaoke bar. You know it? Well, anyway, it's a big night and I get home about 4 a.m. Masako's like that, she doesn't mind if you're a bit late turning up, to give her her due. I was pretty wasted, so I don't remember a whole lot, but I crash out and then Masako and the girl go off in the morning. I'm out to it. Next thing I know there's someone at the door. I try lying low, but the person does not go away and the knocking is echoing through my head, so I check the time. It's nearly midday and I think maybe it's Masako home early from work without her key, though that isn't like her. My head is pounding. I get up and pull on my trousers.' Jun looks up into the eyes of his supposed listener, who takes what appears to be a thoughtful sip from his drink in order to break this imploring stare. Rather sheepishly, Jun resumes his story, 'Yeah I'd have to say I was not feeling at all happy. She was going to get a slap! Anyhow, I open the door and there's this woman there, well-dressed, quite elegant, seemed like I might have seen her before, but my head was in no fit state to remember where. I settle for the idea that she is perhaps one of Masako's friends. 'She's not in,' I say before the woman has a chance to start her spiel. I have the door almost closed as she says, 'Mr. Oyamada, it is you I have this package for' and she takes this big envelope from her bag and hands it to me. 'Thanks,' I say, 'but I have to get back to bed... night shift,' I say. She nods and smiles, a real cute smile I don't mind admitting, turns and walks away. I admire the view for a second or two, but the sun is so bright it hurts my eyes. And then...' The bar door opens. A young couple peer in. The woman asks 'Is this your dog? We gave him a drink of water. I hope you don't mind.' The look of incomprehension on Jun's face is matched by that on the bar-owner's.

Sardinas en Salsa de Tomate.
I shall pause here and try to describe to you the flavour of the sauce the sardines were in. Definitely piquant, that's for sure. The flavour of the fish had diffused through it, creating what I can only say was an almost malty sweetness which persisted even after I drank the water.

You do indeed seem to have acquired quite a taste for sardines in tomato sauce... Go on.

Dog Days.
'You didn't say what was in the package,' says the bar-owner. 'Well, first off I crashed right back to bed to give my head time to catch up with the day, but that wasn't going to work. I'm just lying there trying to figure out if I'd seen the woman before, and where.' The bar-owner breaks away for a moment to turn up the music system. Alejandro Escovedo is playing 'Miss You'. Jun barely hears the music. His own story is running on in his head. 'After a while, I hear the girl come home and I hear her making noodles for herself in the kitchen.' The bar-owner looks to the rapidly cooling bowl on the bar. Jun does not notice this glance. 'So I get up, have a shower and get dressed, and then I check the package and it's a silver necklace with a kind of cylinder thing hanging from it. It doesn't mean anything to me and it's not Masako's style in jewellery at all, so if she finds it there'll be trouble, as I'm sure you can imagine. Luckily, I have a cunning idea; I figure I'll give it to the girl—I'd forgotten her birthday the

previous month, anyway. Yep, always an upside, that's me. So I take it to her room where she's eating noodles. She's on her phone, of course, but I get a smile from her and she mouths 'thanks' at me while slurping her noodles. That's about all the thanks you're going to get from kids nowadays. Anyway, a bit later Masako gets home. She's pretty tired from her day at work, but she's a pearl and pretty soon she sets about getting the evening meal. Just when I figure the day is about to settle, the kid starts screaming. She rushes out of her room, she's crying and screaming... I grab my knife and in I go, ready for anyone, I can tell you. There's nobody there. Then I see it — she has unscrewed the cylinder halves and there on the desk is a wriggling maggot-larva thing. It's a kind of sick, cheesy-white colour with a line of red dots along each side of its body, a metallic blue head and what I think at the time is a greeny-black anus. And it seems to be growing! Well, of course, I smash it, but you know men can never do things right these days and before I even realise it she's back in the room and screaming all over again that I have ruined her homework 'cos I've splattered the guts of the thing all over it. I try telling the girl that now the thing's out of the cylinder she can keep all her secrets there. Masako is not impressed. She thinks I've done it to give the kid a scare. So I think, to hell with it, I'm never going to do anything right, so I get the fuck out, making sure to slam the door as I go. But you can be sure I know it's me that somebody's got it in for, not them! Anyway, I give it a couple of days to let things cool down before I go round to Masako's place again—to check how she is, see. Well, I can tell the girl is home right off — she's got that K-pop shit blaring — and then I see it. It looks just like the first one, this package at the door, and it's addressed to Masako. I'm not paranoid, but I'm thinking this is not good, it isn't likely to be in my interest for Masako to open this package. I pinch it pretty damn quick, I don't mind saying.'

The bar-owner mutters something which Jun fails to catch. He stares into the now cold and unappetizing bowl of noodles, picks up the chopsticks and nudges the food around the bowl, puts them down, and returns to his story.

'I dump the package in a rubbish bin at the train station. Lots of people milling about, but I know where there's a blind spot on the surveillance cameras and then I figure why not just get out of the city for a few days—country air and all that, so I take the next train to leave the station. But nothing ever runs smoothly in my life and I've barely stepped off the train at the end of the line and just my luck, I run into Shimizada and he's asking me how Masako is, how the girl is, what I'm up to, the usual shit. He always did ask too many questions. At one time, I had him down for a nark, but really he's just a stupid person. Anyway, to fob him off I ask if he's got anything on and he says he has some pachinko machines that need shifting. Well, I'm your man, I say. I figure after a couple of days' work I'll be flush and go back to Masako's, maybe take her out to dinner, and things will be sweet. And I do that. Well, almost. She's bitching that a copy of some famous stories she ordered has not been delivered and that the courier company are insisting it has. I say perhaps it was stolen She gives me a funny look and says perhaps. But in the end we do go out to dinner and things are good between us. In the morning, she's gone to work before I wake and the girl is at school, so I've got the place to myself. I figure I'm going to have a pretty stress-free day. How wrong can you be? Anyway, I cruise through the day, have the odd drink... you know how it is.'

The bar-owner looks directly at him. 'I'm here seven days a week,' he says.

'Right. But the thing is, see, that late in the day I'm in the hallway and I get a glimpse of a woman going into the bedroom.

At first I think it's Masako, but then I realise this woman is taller, so I'm thinking maybe I have left the door open and, anyway, what's she going into the bedroom for? So I creep down the hall and sneak a look in. The woman is undressing. Maybe she's the woman from the visit the other day, but then I'm not looking too closely at her face. I hear Masako coming in. She's talking to the girl. I panic. She's coming down the hall. I can't let her go in—it will end things, so I... and then the girl, she's screaming. And in a glance I see that the mysterious woman is no longer in the room.'

The bar-owner does not betray the slightest surprise, simply saying, 'I'm shutting up, you'll have to shove off.'

This murderer, this Jun, he grumbles about having nowhere to go.

He is right; it is a cold night. We sleep under a bridge.

The next morning, I follow him around the city until he enters a work-wear store. I suspect he is trying to find some kind of disguise. And indeed I am right, for at the moment he comes out of the store in new green and grey clothes I almost do not recognize him. But then the same acrid smells of stale human sweat, unwashed feet, rancid desperation and alcohol fumes slough off the figure and I know I still have my man. So I follow him through the market where, ever true to type, he steals a banana from the fruit stall of the woman with the withered arm.

So then, as I said, I discovered the scent of a bitch and followed it, but it was my misfortune that it ended at a high-rise block.

Ahh — slings and arrows! But what do Adam and Eve have to do with your tale?

Clip-clop.

The dreaming woman wakes. 'I was dreaming,' she says. 'I had to wake up to see if I'd died,' she says.

'I,' says Adam. He is a man of few words. The next step is to either repeat himself or halt. However, after their triumphant success at the ball, he and Eve were invited by the eternally youthful Petya Perov to Christmas at the Ivanovs'. They are eagerly awaited. We have this information on the very good authority of the dog, Vera. Emma Bovary may also have been invited.

Now, there is a bitch! That Vera — what a name! Vera of 'Dulcinea is dead. Everywhere, bloody spots. What black manners' and so on, that Vera indeed, though if I were you, I should put this aside for the moment. You have not outlined what it was that interested the blind woman in the sordid affair of the murderer.

Clip-clop.

Sancho: 'Bad tidings, I fear. And who are these Ivanovs? I ask.'

The Like of it Now Happens.
My mistress, who I might say so far as a dog might be concerned, is merely an adequate mistress, aims to perfect the art of asking a question. Life, may just go blap and that is that, she says, but a perfectly asked question will ring through time forever. For example, she asks—if space and time are emergent, then perhaps it is the singularities, should they exist, that are our boundaries. Now, you may be sure that I am unable to answer this. After all, I am a dog and have no need to concern

myself whether or not this may be fictively or factually true. I lead and the blind woman follows. That is all. Of course, you may be sure, as I have already intimated, I follow when she commands. But it is true that her vision is turned completely inward and from somewhere inside her she is able to see into other humans. Perhaps this is a ninth sense? She also loves music, which is, as you may know, a very strange arrangement of sounds. But there is something else which I feel I ought to report. I have carefully watched many singers and I am now almost certain that she responds not only to the music but also to the actual state of the singers when they turn inward to await the moment in the music where all the sounds cross-hatch to their point of clarity. I have seen this myself, though it meant nothing to me. The woman who is about to sing is paused. The men, who have little machines on their heads, (maybe that is how they are filled with music?) thrash some other machines and in the next instant the woman transforms, sinks into herself and lets the song pour out of her.
I have also seen other humans sink into themselves, but no music comes from them—they simply die.

Your tale is becoming somewhat tangled. You should return it to a dream, or maybe attempt to convey that it has some utility like that of the woman who retails her experiences.

I can tell of my life and experience, but I am not certain that that would not be the ruin of them. For instance, let me tell you about my jousts with the water thief that lives in our courtyard. It drips day and night. If I drink from it, my mistress scolds me. She shouts that I am stealing her time. I cannot for the life of me understand how the thing continues to drip for so long. I am absolutely certain that there is no dog who might compete with it. My mistress, her name is Kleio by the way, is always quick to have the handyman fix the dripping taps as well as the drains when they block. It is things like this dripping which create my difficulty in being certain of what it is that is true.

Clip-clop.

Also, the courtyard encloses a goldfish pond. I often wonder what story a goldfish might tell. I have, from time to time, dipped a paw into the pond to chase these little fish, but they are too quick. Maybe they see my paw as a sign that I am one of their gods chivvying them along.
Anyhow, the courtyard is covered with flagstones between which a crazing of dark green moss grows. I have my suspicions that there is something hidden beneath these stones. Some years ago, the handyman dropped a log on the flagstones and I heard a low hollow reverberation coming from deep underground.
I once heard two old women gossiping behind the fence of the alley which runs behind our courtyard. They were talking about a child who vanished many years ago. One of the women was the pug-faced person from the house with the big tree, and here I shall simply observe that it is easier for a dog than an old person to be touched—except by madness. But to return to my mistress, I know that some other humans are aware that she has this thing, this... I grasp for words... inside her, and that they are wary of it, though I do not precisely know why.

Forgive me but, to go back for a moment, I meant to ask: What was the reaction of the girl on seeing the body of her mother?

I will never forget — all the music drained from her in one scream.

Ahh... well... I can only say that sometimes my role as interlocutor casts this dog into dark corners.

Allow me to return to Adam and Eve. I might first mark their unfitness for this particular tale. Somehow, they are at once the first people and the descendants of the Mesopotamian gods—ornaments stolen from other people's histories. Now they have become mere celebrities who float from event to event—eternally ageless, eternally lost, unlike Marmaduke, whose greatest danger is that of having his own greed elbow him into the oblivion he so dreads.

I too am an old dog — how this happened I do not know. It seems to me to be more than time simply passing. Maybe I am running out of words. Maybe I will die. We all will die. But will I be a mad dog before I die? That is my question.

I have no answer. I can only continue this story of my own life. Some years ago, I heard my mistress tell the neighbour that as a small girl she was once roundly chastised for having left the rice on the school bus. Then, in some odd twist in her train of thought, she added that her favourite movie of all time was *Arigato-san* and she went on to describe the journey of that bus and its hero, which I think she regarded as a modern version of some ancient tale of heroic struggle—a journey story.

True, perhaps, though I also detect the ring of an exemplary story.

That may well prove to be the case.

Clip-clop.

That neighbour was the neighbour whose boy was often sent to help my mistress, a quite intelligent boy, but a boy my mistress had to constantly chide to get rather simple tasks done properly. The kid would stop and read anything. My mistress, who had been for some years a teacher, never became angry with him. This surprised me. He deserved a kick at the very least, but she would say to me, under her breath almost, and certainly out of his hearing, 'At least he reads. He will make good sooner or later.'

I do not know what became of him, but the neighbour died. Their house sat empty for a time, after which a new woman, younger and quite beautiful, moved in. I truly do not know what my mistress's thoughts about her are, but she is popular with the men in this street of ours. She has slow moving eyes.

Indeed, we dogs can tell of many such things!

Certainly—but there are also the other people with whom we continue to pass the moments of a lifetime. They constantly float with us in the turmoil of our minds, in the roiling turbulence of our thoughts, always returning to the surface unsullied, undiminished, forever with us. I shall stop now before strange thoughts and alien footprints begin to muddle my tale.

My apologies. Forgive me for throwing you an old bone.

Not at all. There is nothing wrong with an old bone, if properly seasoned.

Bravo! Please continue.

Clip-clop.

I must confess I have somewhat lost the scent of my story. I do believe a storyteller should be able to generate the illusion that they have something to say and to have lost the thread of your own life, well…

I find that without this 'true' point of reference, the unity of my life decays before me and, in turn, strangles the re-telling of my experiences.

Perhaps that is the fate of all we shaggy dogs. You have come face to face with a solid fact of imagination. You were, as I recall, in your mistress's courtyard.

Ah yes, about the sculpture in the garden alcove. It is an ugly little man. A squat, ugly little man, in fact. Moreover, he is a squat, ugly little man with an erect penis. This penis comes level with his chin. He is sitting on a partially carved stool. I have never liked this figure and have made my disdain plain! What, I ask myself, of the workmen who hewed the stone in the quarry then struggled to haul it to the sculptor's studio where that same sculptor carefully and deliberately erased, ablated, excised all trace of them and their efforts? Should they not have their record also? Would they not have preferred that that block of stone be a stool for them to retire to and sit upon at the extremity of their labours?

You make a valid point. I am quite familiar with a number of statues of this kind.

My mistress also has a small Zen garden which, when the mood takes her, she tends with great care. It gives me pleasure to watch her working with her old wooden tools. I see the dreamy satisfaction on her face as she strokes the chattering stones or her hand caresses the moss-covered rocks.

And now, as these stones chatter in my mind, I recall a curious event. Some years ago, a strange thing occurred. My mistress produced from the wooden bucket in which she keeps some of her garden tools a rag. It had the strong scent of a human I had never come into contact with before. She gave me a small, sealed package and, of course, I understood she wanted me to deliver this package to this person whom I took from their scent to be an older person with some, to my nose, indefinable illness. Our town is not small, but by forgoing the areas I knew well and working with the breezes I soon set up a systematic pattern for my search and began working it. After several hours, the search began to narrow to the valley on the far side of the town and I worked my way steadily up it. At the head of the valley, where I am sure water had to be carried uphill for several hundred metres, there was situated an old shack from which the same rag spoor emanated. I dared not bark for fear of dropping the package so I set it down as gently as I could. My approach had gone unnoticed; no sounds of stirring came from the shack. The battered old door seemed jammed in the arc of dirt it described in consequence of its topmost hinge being broken. And without any better plan I began to howl and bark, for it was a hot day and I had no wish to spend unnecessary moments in the full heat of the west-facing valley. Eventually, a figure shuffled to the door, with some difficulty wrenched it open and stood blinking in the strong light, though it seemed oblivious to the heat of the day. When the figure spotted me, I proffered the package which I had retrieved. After a moment, the figure, it seemed to be an old man, noticed it and took it from me. He examined the package for a moment before breaking the seal and fishing out a paper from which he read aloud to himself in a quavering and rather mystified voice.

'North-west of zero, south-west of Priapus, under earth and

sun lies Petya Petrov.' The old man looked to me and said, as if raising a great confidence, 'Who is this Petya Petrov? I know of no Petya Petrov, the woman must be mad. I have only one son, and he was lost to me long ago.' He turned away. I did not see what else was in the package.

I went over to a nearby tree and marked my ascent and then the tiredness of my day's search overcame me and I made haste to descend the valley and find water and shade—this dog is not a dog to lie for long in the sun.

Indeed, a nap, though brief, provides ease for a weary mind and body. For all that, I now sense your stories, these things about which you are telling, swirling together. I assume that the old man was once the husband of your mistress—and this Jun, their son?

Clip-clop.

I do recall once hearing my mistress observe, 'My son, he is a weed'. As for husband? All I can say for certain is that that old man was no more than a void in the fabric of the universe. I, for one, have no opinion as to how anyone should live. After all, life has proceeded for millennia and it is quite apparent and no longer worthy of advice or discussion how each should live their own. Neither is it worthy of report yet, alas, here I am. My mistress, who reads with her fingers, has often said to me (having flung aside some book or other) that a proper book or story can bear any question, that every book should set its own terms and be 'evermore faithful to them'.

I note your concern. Between us, we shall try and resolve this story. I will ask some questions of you. Does your mistress ever go out without you?

Yes, indeed. She takes the screaming stick with her. I do not mind, as I must confess that I enjoy the peacefulness that comes over the house, though sometimes the kids and their bash-boom-bang on the fences in the back alley are an annoying interruption to the peace and quiet of the house.

Does your mistress ever take packages with her on these occasions?

I cannot say so for certain. She does seem to enjoy creating parcels. I have watched the concentration on her face as she wraps and ties and by the way she feels and touches her handiwork then applies her seal to it. I am sure she gains a great deal of pleasure from the process.

Had you ever heard her speak of Jun?

Never.

We are left to ponder: Did this Jun, perhaps, not recognize his own mother, and why? Is there some other Jun? Let's leave that. I shall try another approach. Had you and your mistress on any prior occasion been at the place in the street where you heard the scream?

I'm sure we must have been. We walk a lot, though we certainly had not been there recently.

Well, I suppose we can only conclude that murder mysteries by their very nature always contain holes. Similarly, it is always a lesser character, at first seen only tangentially, who proves to be of great significance, though not, as in this case, so often the actual murderer.

Clip-clop.

Have we addressed that case? Should I continue?

That is not necessary. You have done well. The story is told. We can sidle away thinking our own thoughts as we go.

It is raining outside. The translator looks up from the final page. The saccadic/ergodic style of the book has proved taxing. She wouldn't wish it on a reader encumbered with a withered attention span. What to make of it? With her hands she sweeps her hair from her forehead, eases her chair away from her desk then stands, still pondering her own question. Her friend, coming into the room, sees her uncertainty, comes to her and holds her. The translator sighs. 'I'm okay, it's the way it's done... Sometimes I wonder whether it is better for a book to have its genesis in a small language or in the far, far exurbs of the tower of dross generated in English.' She laughs quietly to herself as she gently breaks the embrace of her friend.
'How pompous I sound. What does better mean?'

Clip-clop.

'But then, I do need the work.'

Don Quixote: All is folly, Sancho, pure folly.

KIREJI WITH SALT AND MAUNDER

Lying here is boring. Nothing to do—wander around in my own head. Is it my head? Treacherous stomach. Pancreas? I'm dying.

First things first. Went to the doctor not so long ago. Could almost have whistled on my way in but for these bloody dentures. Click-clack. Not a care in the world. Just a check-up, they said. And here I am… in this bloody bed. Too late now. Should never have gone there. Serves me right.

Alopecia, alopecia, jonty alopecia, alopecia, jetter plumeray. Too old for all that now. And 'Greensleeves'. Damn window's too high. Somebody's idea of a joke — all I can see are little white clouds pootling by. Or grey. Plenty of time to watch them when I've gone. Or maybe I'm down the other end? I stare out of the window to see birds pass by, a little game, but they dive past and I can't be sure whether I saw them or not.

There's a spider on the far wall, a daddy long legs. Some kid said if their fangs were bigger… and I said if their jaws were bigger they'd rip your head off. Shut him up. A born second-rater. Of course no one ever said that. They don't, do they, nonetheless—you know. Third, you'd be oblivious! Going to hell? Books don't fare too well there, so nothing to read, but the booze is probably better. Religious twaddle. Grow up. Bit late for that.

Thought I saw a plane yesterday. Heard nothing. Double glazing, I guess. The nurse, she's efficient — throws me round like a piece of meat, tries to be nice. Don't like her. Had a kapok bed once—lay in it surrounded on all sides. And an eiderdown. All sealed in with pillows. Not this plank. Probably makes it easy for them. You're all stretched out nice and tidy. This is the death cell — three have gone since I got in here.

School swimming pool, bloody freezing — learning to swim when we could have just climbed out! Wouldn't mind a whisky, with a little splash, just to smooth the wrinkles. Cast and fly blown, that's me.

Dozed off there.

My water's warm... and stale. Ring the bell? Can't be bothered. Turn over. Wouldn't mind a curried egg sandwich. Not the lettuce and Vegemite I struggled to get through at primary school. Dutifully eaten. What a good boy. And the sun-warmed milk. Now I'm lying here on my belly like a wrinkled old lizard on a sun-warmed rock. Not like the old days. Discovered we could go from the fence on one side of our place across the garage and house roof to the fence on the other. Two-storey it was, too. Mum stayed calm when she saw us—probably thought we'd fall if she shouted. More like a ferret in those days.

Thought for a minute there were flashes of lightning outside, but it's just the bloody light in the car park coming on. Someone should change the bulb in the bloody thing; flickers all night, keeping all the decent dying folk awake. Probably buzzes, too.

Grandma had a terrier called Scottie. Odd, that. Maybe she wrote it 'Scotty'. No need to worry, no need to write it down. Turn onto my side. This tube's a damned nuisance. Pretty much said I wasn't worth an op, so I drew the line at chemo and here I am. Somebody down the corridor's snoring again. Strange how when you're like this everyone's giving you room, space, letting you be yourself and expecting you'll want to heal yourself, as if the last thing they want is you to be with them as you are, as you've always been, though they never before seemed to notice you as you are. Still, no matter. They can discuss that before the sandwiches and savouries come around—and sort out the marks for your performance.

You might be, just once, remembered for something you said to a friend. But that friend died!

Now I'd swear there's a strange, furtive sort of noise at the end of the bed. Must be my toenails growing. I'll go and they'll carry on, at least till Fryday. Bit grim there. Must try harder, as the school report always said. They keep this place so bloody cold, probably trying to make you stay in bed. Went for a walk this morning, managed to get up for a piss, wheeled the tube-stand thing with me, took ages. Just corridors. Captured at the lobby flower stand. Seeing all those flowers, that was worth it! Can still see them with my eyes closed. Had a good garden once. Never mind that now, try and get some sleep.

Loud crash! Someone's dropped a dinner tray in the corridor.

Mine's sitting on the bed table. Still warm—wonder of wonders. Don't feel like it. Wander back into my dreams. Suppose I always was a watcher, stood too far back, not showing off, avoiding the limelight. A little sip from the miniatures and on to quietly becoming a paralytic converter—that's a joke. Life can be cruel, like the sound of a rusty iron gate squealing shut.

Dad insisted that (after his death) I deliver a book he owned. He got it from somebody who had already died. Biked way out of town. The bloke was a bit mystified, said he already had a copy.

Silence. It's such strange stuff. There's this sterile, medical version, and there's the sudden thundering silence that follows a loud explosion. And what of the intake of breath and silence that follows a great shock or unexpectedly delivered shard of truth when all would probably be better served by a prescription—no going in to the doctor, just an eternal sojourn in the waiting room. Bit like here without the machines. Wheels squeaking in the corridor.

Fell asleep for a moment. Well, I think so; the dinner's gone.

Wee-wah, wee-wah — police sirens cutting through the double glazing. Exotic scenery in the background. High drama. The chase, the romance, the thrill of it all. Cut, change scenery. Low key, that's the thing, serious questions about life, change scenery, cut, that's the heaving bosom of the story! Not much to say. This is not my life. I'm dreaming. I'm dying. Went to the quack... Wee-wah, Wee-wah. Cut, change scenery.

My seal is livid. Why am I thinking that? Doesn't make sense. Prehistory of words. I'll make a movie, *Hitman's Day*—cheap motel room — bleak walls, sparse furniture, doubtfully-made bed — stains, very little decoration except a generic print of a nondescript alley in a non-existent city. A random sign from the Chinese whispers school of art. Close-up of clock. Ten-thirty, hard to tell whether it's day or night. Nobody in the room until the camera slowly tilts down to the floor and shows us the spread-eagled body in the pool of blackening blood. It's the hitman. His luck ran out. And now you hear the flies.

Stupid idea. Grow up. No time for that now. Funny the way things go. You think time flows, but really it lurches. My life's gone this fast, but I can't tell it at the same speed — irreducibly inexpressible, that's it.

Turnips! She's telling me turnips are exceedingly nutritious. There is nothing wrong with eating them. Many people do not like them, but she cannot help that. Turnip fibre sweeps the gut clean. That is a well-known fact. A clean gut is essential for a successful life. She drinks two litres of turnip milk a day to help her keep 'totally hydrated'. Quite how they milk turnips she has no idea. The information on the carton assures the prospective purchaser that it is done humanely and that turnip milk, when diligently applied (as per the label) also rehydrates and soothes the skin after exposure to strong sunlight. And it repels mosquitoes! The label goes on to say that the user should not apply turnip milk before going into the hot sun as it has an SPF of minus three. She assures me that she has seen evidence for this. The picture showed an 'actual' turnip growing in the wild, or wherever it is that turnips 'actually' grow. She was surprised to learn that they grow in 'actual' dirt, as she had been assured by her best friend on social media that they are sea vegetables like cucumbers. She does sometimes make turnip and cucumber smoothies (her secret is that she includes a lettuce leaf as well, as this adds to her daily green vege quota). Anyway, she says, this 'actual' picture of an 'actual' turnip 'actually' growing, showed that the turnip had bad skin colour where it had been in the sun.
She first found out about the amazing benefits of turnips when a friend of hers on social media, not the previous one, a different one, though they're no longer friends 'cos she blocked her,

'the skank'! This friend had tried to tell her that it was true that they test turnip medicines on gerberas. Why would they do that? she asked. Gerberas are so cuddly. Turnip fries go best with chilli dipping sauce, or lemon and mint.

She shows me the matching turnip tattoos on her inner thighs. She had researched and discovered that hardly any famous people have conspicuous turnip tatts. Perhaps I am one of the first turnip influencers, she says, adding that an amazing fact about turnips is that they are now definitely known to be 'totally' gluten free. She has even heard that there are different kinds of turnips. Some are endangered! As an influencer, she has her own line of jewellery — nine carat turnip charms and necklace fobs. She saw on social media that there is a company which plans to produce turnip fibre yarn. If she had a 'way bigger allowance' she would have bought the shares they were advertising, as she thinks a turnip clothing range of her own would be 'way cool'.

She says it will not be long before her range of turnip flavoured instant noodles will be in supermarkets and that turnip powder could be used in making ice-cream and gelato, which, she says, is Italian for ice-cream. Big companies, though, are beginning to get in on the turnip thing and there are imports from foreign countries as well, although she saw somewhere that foreign turnip products, which are 'way cheap', contain foreign substances, nasty additives and stuff like that and you can't even eat them 'cos they make your innards get all clogged and icky.

Who the fuck is this woman? Why am I dreaming this? Nurse! I need to pee.

Damned television, stuck on the same damned channel, same damned drama. I'm watching it backwards, seen it so often

— doesn't make any sense, need a conversation, a quiet chat, with the actress. Your eyes, I'd say, they chose you for your eyes. They chose you for your challenging gaze, your stare through the screen, defying the audience, defying the plot, standing only for you, the character, and the fact that it's you — you, the actress. They all say their lines, but still, you have the eyes. Now a horde of actresses accost me, all demanding to know if they were you... And, marching from somewhere in the recesses of my brain, Hollywood, Hollywood, would, would, would'ja, Holly would you be my friend? Now there's a tune!

A visitor. Are you all right? she asks. Yes, I say. Dying is pretty much just an accident of birth, I say. No flowers. They'll come later, I guess. Home-made biscuits. Anzac, click-clack. Hum. Drone. Felt like saying, look, Adrienne, while you are sitting there talking about your grand-kids, grand-kids I've never met, you do realize, don't you, that gravity is having it off with your arse?

Picked cocksfoot along the roadsides, sixpence a pound, bit dusty when the cars came by. Here's the nurse come to give me and Stumpy a sponge bath. Very professional—not so much as a twitch out of him.

Christ! It's on for young and old. The nurse's accomplice - the fingernail, toenail, nose, eyebrow and ear hair trimmer - invites herself into the room. I'll try a new tactic this time; let her do her worst then give her two hundred and tell her she's half way to becoming a lawyer. Shock treatment!

Too much excitement—I'll doze for a little while. Nice to have a little patch of sun on the bedspread. Probably an oversight when they designed this dump. Tried reading the book again, but the stuffing kept falling out of it.

Forty winks. Forty thieves.

Old age really is a different universe. Hell, even the universe can't abide it, leaves black holes around to tidy things up! The good thing about dying is that you're somewhat, more or less, excused—you no longer have to get up and go through the motions of living.

Why did I write the book, this book the stuffing keeps falling out of? All that's been said and thought before—not much room left here. Just doing it for my own amusement, bemusement? No need to argue over who might have said what or why. I offer you my salutations and hope you may be one of those people fortunate enough to be unaware that you have died. I've no idea what time it is, gets lost in here. Next Thurs

Clip-clop.